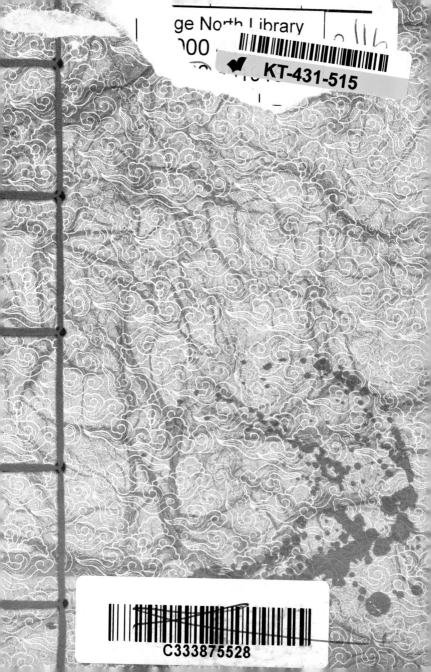

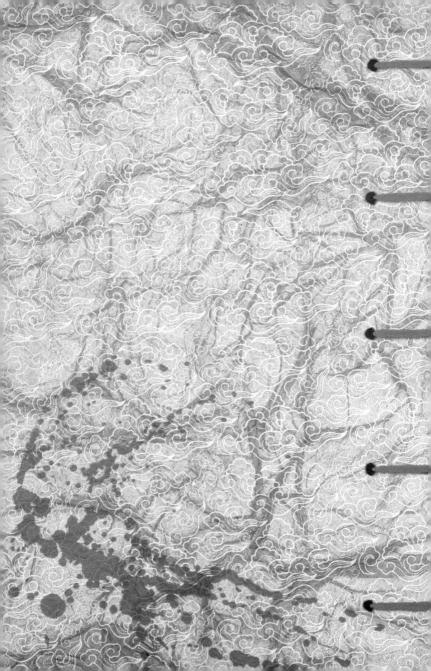

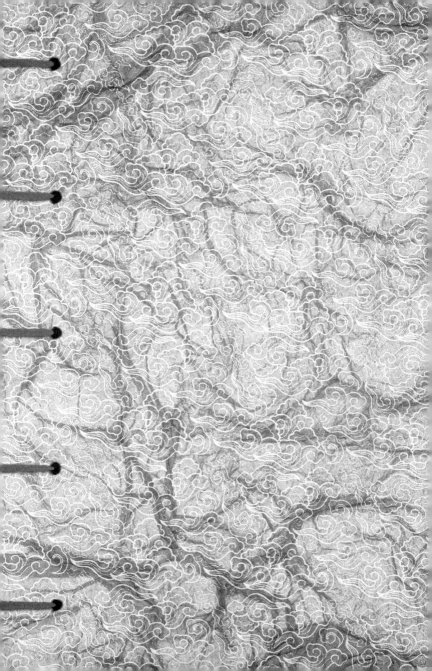

SHADOW WARRIORS

Conkers

First published in 2016 in Great Britain by
Barrington Stoke Ltd
18 Walker Street, Edinburgh, EH3 7LP

www.barringtonstoke.co.uk

A CIP catalogue record for this book is available
from the British Library upon request

ISBN: 978-1-78112-551-9

Printed and bound by CPI Group (UK) Ltd, Croydon, CR0 4YY

CHRIS BRADFORD

SHADOW WARRIORS

With illustrations by
DAVID WYATT

onkers

To Leo, my little ninja

1. Black Belt Test

Japan, Year 1580

I wait **under** the floorboards.

I've been hidden here for over an hour, lying still as a stone.

My name is Taka. This is my first mission as a ninja and I must not fail.

I hear a door slide open and look through the crack in the floorboards. I watch as a man crosses the room. His feet pass close to my face. He wears a gold silk robe with the crest of a black eagle on his back. He carries two samurai swords on his hip. Across his right cheek is a long red scar.

It's Lord Oda – the samurai warrior I've been waiting for.

The warlord doesn't know I'm here. He can't see me under the floor. He sits down on his bed. In his hand, he holds a scroll of paper. He begins to read it.

"I never dreamed such things were possible," he mutters to himself.

After a few minutes, he puts the scroll into a wooden

box by his pillow. He lays his swords beside his bed, blows out the candle and goes to sleep.

Outside, a full moon has risen over the castle. Its pale light shines through a small window and onto the cruel face of Lord Oda. Lord Oda is the sworn enemy of the ninja. My task is to stop him destroying our clan.

Now is the time.

I push softly at the loose floorboard above me and climb out of my hiding place. Using my ninja stealth skills, I cross the room without a sound. In the darkness I'm almost invisible. My black clothes and my hood turn me into a shadow. Only my eyes show.

As I draw close to the samurai lord, I see my hands are shaking.

'Can I really do this?' I ask myself.

I've been training to be a spy and an assassin all my life. But I'm still only fourteen. Have I learned all the skills I need for this mission? Perhaps I should have waited for Cho.

Can I save our ninja clan all on my own?

I have to prove myself. Tonight.

I'm now so close to Lord Oda, I can hear him breathe. As I reach out, my arm blocks the moonlight shining onto his face.

A small but fatal mistake.

Lord Oda's eyes snap open. For a moment, we stare at each other in shock.

Then he screams, "GUARDS!"

The Day Before ...

Holding the silver *shuriken* in my right hand, I take aim and flick the throwing star at the target. It flashes through the air like a mini bolt of lightning.

I've been practising
with this weapon every
day, but even I can't
believe it when the *shuriken* strikes the tree
trunk dead centre.

"Very impressive," says Sensei Shima as
he walks over to me in the forest. "That's five
out of five."

I bow to my teacher and kneel back
in line with the other ninja students in the
forest. A girl with long black hair smiles at
me – Cho. She's a year older than me, and her
acrobatic skills are the best in the clan.

"Well done, you even beat Renzo!" she
whispers, looking over at a large sixteen-year-
old boy with strong arms and a shaven head.

Renzo is glaring at me. He never comes second and he doesn't like it.

"It doesn't count," he grunts.

"Why not?" I protest.

"You're not a real ninja. You haven't gone on a mission yet."

Renzo loves to tell me this fact, and all my joy at mastering the Five Blades *shuriken* throw vanishes.

"You're just jealous," says Cho.

"Taka was lucky, that's all," snorts Renzo. "The *real* test is if he can do it under the pressure of a mission."

Sensei Shima claps for attention. "Time for unarmed combat practice," he calls. "Find a partner."

I look to Cho, but Renzo's already at my side, towering over me.

"I pick you," he snarls.

Before I can react, he grabs me by both arms. I try to shake off his grip, but he's too strong. Renzo throws me to the ground. I fight to get back up, but he drops on top of me and pins my arm down with his knee. I groan in pain as he presses with all his weight.

"Just as I thought." He grins and twists my arm so that the pain is almost too much to bear. "You wouldn't survive long in a real fight."

I'm forced to submit. I tap the floor.

"Change opponents!" orders Sensei Shima.

As I get up, I rub my hurt arm. It throbs.

Cho comes over to partner me. "Are you all right?" she asks.

I nod. My arm's fine – it's my pride that's been hurt. I'll never gain the respect of the others until I've completed my first mission.

"He's too strong for me," I answer.

"Everyone has a weak point," replies Cho. "I may be small, but few can beat me."

Without warning, she drives her thumb into the space behind my collarbone. A blinding pain shoots through my body, my legs go weak, and I fall to the ground.

"That's the Dragon's Gate." She smiles. "It's a pressure point that will take down the biggest and ugliest foe."

"Will you show me again?" I ask.

Cho repeats the move. Then she lets me try it on her. I press down and she collapses like a rag doll.

"Sorry, was that too hard?" I ask as I offer my hand to help her up.

"No, it was perfect," she replies. Then she grabs my wrist and, with a quick twist, throws me onto my back. "But that's the last time I'll let you win so easily."

"Stop training!" commands Sensei Shima.

Our clan leader, Tenshin, is walking towards us from the direction of the village. He's wearing his black *gi*, a ninja uniform with the crest of two hawks on the front. The two hawks are the emblem of the clan.

"We need all available ninja for an important mission," says Tenshin.

At last, here's my chance!

I jump to my feet.

"Not you, Taka," Tenshin tells me. "This is a black-belt-only mission."

"This will be my tenth mission," brags Renzo the next morning as the ninja team get ready to leave. "Tell me again, how many have you done, Taka?"

I ignore him and get on with filling everyone's water bottles from the village well.

"You haven't even passed the Grandmaster's black belt test!" Renzo sneers. "Are you sure you can even do water duty on your own?"

12

My face goes red with shame as the other ninja try to hide their laughter.

The Grandmaster is the head of *ninjutsu*, the secret martial art of the ninja. When a student turns fourteen, the Grandmaster invites them to his temple to take a flower from his hand – without being detected. The Grandmaster must feel nothing, must not know they are even there. He is old and blind, but the task is far from easy. There are traps set all through the temple.

It's the ultimate test of stealth for a ninja.

Sensei Shima is the only ninja to have passed the test first time and that was ten years ago. Once a ninja earns their black belt, they're ready to be sent on any mission.

I've failed twice already. Am I ever going to succeed and get my black belt?

As I hand out the water bottles, I watch as my fellow ninja complete their final equipment checks.

How I wish I could go too! But I see that Cho isn't among them. Then I spot her crossing the village square towards me.

"The Grandmaster has asked for you," she says.

I stare at Cho. "Me? But why?"

"Why do you think?" Cho replies, grinning.

"Black belt test!" I exclaim. "But I'm not ready for it."

Renzo overhears us and gives a cruel

laugh. "Those who fail to prepare, must prepare to fail!"

"Don't listen to him," says Cho as we walk away. "I've seen you practising every day. You're ready."

We cross the paddy fields, enter the forest and follow a path up into the mountains. As we draw near to the temple, I get more and more nervous.

"What if I fail again?" I ask Cho.

"Don't worry, it took me two attempts," she replies.

"But this is my third!"

Cho stops and looks at me. "I'll tell you a secret. As strong and skilful as Renzo is, it took him *five* attempts to get his black belt –

not the two he brags about."

This news makes me feel better. But I'm still worried about my chances.

We climb a long flight of stone steps that lead up to a huge wooden gate. Cho stops before the temple entrance.

"I'll meet you later in the village," she says.

"Aren't you going on the mission?" I ask.

Cho shakes her head.

"But I thought all the ninja were going," I say.

"I've been chosen by the Grandmaster for a special task," she tells me before she heads back down the steps. As I pluck up the courage to enter the temple, she calls out, "Good luck! And watch out for that second step."

2. Grandmaster

I pass through the gate and into the temple's courtyard. In front of me is a large open square of grey gravel. On the other side is the temple – a tall wooden pagoda with a spire that pokes out of the top like a spear. To my left there's a beautiful rock garden, a mountain stream flowing through it and into a pond.

The place looks empty. But I know the Grandmaster is waiting for me inside the temple.

As I'm about to step onto the gravel, I quickly pull my foot back.

I almost forgot. I must be cautious. This was how I failed my first attempt. The gravel is there to test a ninja's stealth-walking skills. The Grandmaster heard me crunching across the courtyard before I even got close to the temple.

I take three deep breaths to calm myself and I start again. Just like Sensei Shima's lesson, I point my lead foot and I place my toes down first. Bit by bit I step onto that foot, letting the side then the heel touch the ground. This way I make no sound.

Half way across, I head for the rock garden.

I don't want to make the same mistake

I made on my second attempt. As the Grandmaster is blind, his sense of smell, as well as his hearing, is more sensitive. Last time he smelled the rich fertile earth of the paddy fields on my feet. This was another lesson in how to be invisible – a ninja must remove or cover up any smells that might give him away.

I stand in the mountain stream to wash the dust off my feet. Beside me I see there's a juniper bush. I remember the Grandmaster likes to burn juniper wood in the temple, so I pull off some leaves and rub them on my body. The plant's woody smell hides all traces of my scent. Once my feet are dry, I stealth-walk across the rest of the courtyard.

So far, so good.

I enter the temple. Inside, the main hall is cool and dark. A polished wooden floor leads to steps and a platform where the shrine is. At the centre of the temple, a bronze Buddha glistens in the light of two candles.

In front of the shrine, on the platform, sits the Grandmaster.

He is cross-legged on a cushion and his hands rest in his lap. He is so still he could be

a statue. His face is old and wrinkled with a long grey beard. His eyes look straight at me, but see nothing.

In the palm of his right hand is a blood-red flower.

I creep across the room and am almost at the shrine's steps, when I remember Cho's warning.

Watch out for that second step.

I look closely at the step. There's a row of pins sticking out of the wood. They weren't there the last time.

I climb onto the raised platform, jumping over the second step. In just a few more paces, I'll reach the Grandmaster.

I'm so focused on getting to him without making a sound that I almost don't see the second trap. But a glimmer of light, like a spider web caught in the morning sun, alerts me to the danger. A thin cotton thread stretches across the room at ankle height. On one end is a little bell.

I'm now glad for all Sensei Shima's training. In lessons he'd make us walk through the forest looking closely at everything we passed to spot any traps – rocks we could trip over at night, or bushes and trees in which the enemy might hide. He'd tell us, "It's not what you look at, but what you see."

I step over the thread with great care and approach the Grandmaster. I can almost touch the blood-red flower and the Grandmaster still hasn't moved.

I stop for a split second. I can't believe I'm about to earn my black belt. There must be another trap. But I can't see one.

Just as I reach for the flower, the Grandmaster grabs my hand and pain rockets through my body. My body freezes as he presses a nerve point in my wrist.

The Grandmaster turns to me.

"Never assume a man with no eyes
cannot see."

"I'll never be a ninja," I say, and I hang
my head low.

"Your life is an unknown road," replies the Grandmaster, as we walk along a stone path back through the temple garden. "How can you be so sure?"

"But without my black belt, I can't go on a mission."

The Grandmaster turns his blind eyes upon me.

"A black belt is nothing more than a belt that goes around your waist," he says. "Being a black belt is a state of mind. When your mind is ready, then you'll be a black belt."

"But I've failed *three* times," I sigh.

"Failure is success if you learn from it."

"So what did I do wrong?" I ask. "I avoided all your traps."

The Grandmaster smiles. "That you did. But you made three mistakes."

"Three!" I blurt out.

"The first mistake was coming in through the door. A ninja must never do what his enemy expects. Always come from a different direction – the window, the roof, from behind or below. When you came through the door, your sound shadow gave you away."

"My sound shadow?" I ask.

The Grandmaster points to the sun, then to my darkened outline upon the ground. "Like the sun makes a shadow of your body, so it is with sound. As you passed through the door, you blocked the noise of the mountain stream. For a moment, the sound of running water became softer and I knew you had come."

"You noticed *that*?" I say, amazed.

The Grandmaster nods. "Close your eyes. What do you hear?"

"I hear the stream trickling and birds singing."

"Do you hear your own heartbeat?" he asks.

"No."

"Do you hear the ant that is at your feet?"

"No," I reply. I look down and see an ant carrying a leaf across the path. "Grandmaster, how can you hear these things?"

"Taka, how can you not?"

I understand now that the Grandmaster is teaching me an important lesson in how to look and listen. I must watch and listen to *everything* around me.

"Your second mistake was not to match your breathing to my breathing," the Grandmaster says.

I don't understand. "How would that make a difference?" I ask.

"I could sense you as you got closer. You need to be in harmony with your target," he explains. "Remember, for a ninja, a small error is as deadly as a big one. When you jump over a canyon it doesn't matter if you get half way across or miss by an inch, you still fall to your death."

The Grandmaster drops his blood-red flower into the stream.

As I watch it float away, he goes on.
"Your third and final mistake was to let doubt
enter your mind, to become unsure. At the last
moment you stopped for a split second, didn't
you?"

"Yes, Grandmaster," I admit, and I bow
my head in shame. "But I just didn't think I
could do it."

"Always believe in yourself," the
Grandmaster says firmly.

"How can I, when I keep failing?"

"Take your lesson from the ant," replies
the Grandmaster. He points to the insect
still trying to drag the leaf across the stones.
"Whatever the size of the task or the things in
its way, the ant never gives up."

With a last tug, the ant pulls the leaf off the path and carries on with its journey through the grass.

"You see, Taka," says the Grandmaster, resting his hand on my arm. "It doesn't matter how slowly you go, so long as you don't stop."

3. The Scrolls

"Grandmaster!" cries Cho, running through the gateway. "The Scrolls have been stolen!"

We both turn to her in shock. The Scrolls are the secret teachings of the ninja. Written upon them is everything the Grandmaster knows, and all that the Grandmasters before him knew – weapon skills, hand-to-hand fighting methods, the Seven Disguises, the Sixteen Secret Fists, the Death Touch, deadly poisons and even ninja magic.

"What happened?" asks the Grandmaster.

"I visited the Hidden Shrine as you asked," replies Cho, out of breath, "but when I got there it had been attacked."

"What about Monk Osamu who was guarding it?" asks the Grandmaster. On his wise face I see worry for his old friend.

"He's alive but badly beaten."

"Does he know who did this?"

Cho nods. "They were samurai. They wore the black eagle crest of Lord Oda's army."

The Grandmaster gives a deep sigh. "This comes as no surprise."

I clench my fists in anger at the news. For as long as I can remember, Lord Oda has been our enemy. While some samurai hire the ninja as spies and assassins, most do not trust us and a few, like Lord Oda, want to destroy us all. What makes it worse for me is that this samurai lord murdered my father during the Battle of Black Eagle thirteen years ago. Because of him, I never met my father.

"We must get back the Scrolls," the Grandmaster says, slamming his fist into his palm. "Lord Oda must not learn our secrets. If he does, our clan is doomed. He will defeat us. Tell me, when did the attack take place?"

"Early this morning," Cho replies.

"We still have time," the Grandmaster

says. "Black Eagle Castle is a day's march from the Hidden Shrine, but a ninja can speed-run there in half the time. Send our two best ninja at once."

"All our ninja are on a mission," Cho tells him.

The Grandmaster strokes his grey beard, thinking hard. "Cho, you must go alone then. It'll be very dangerous, but –"

"I'll go with Cho," I say.

"This is not a test, Taka," replies the Grandmaster. "You could get killed."

"You told me that being a black belt is a state of mind. That I must believe in myself. Well, I can do this if you give me the chance."

"I know how you feel about Lord Oda,"

the Grandmaster says. "You want to fight him for what he did to your father. But you cannot allow the wish for revenge to take away your focus. That could lead to failure."

"I seek justice, not revenge," I reply. "To get back the Scrolls will be justice."

The Grandmaster stares at me. I know he can't see, but it feels like he's looking deep into my soul.

"So be it," he says with a grave look on his face. "Complete the mission and *nothing* else. The fate of our clan is now in your hands."

4. Black Eagle Castle

I speed-run through the forest, moving like the wind between the trees. Cho is ahead of me. She leaps over a log, as light and fast as a young deer.

We carry almost nothing since we need to be fast. I have my *shuriken* stars in my pack. Cho has a grappling hook on her belt and a sword strapped to her back. We are both dressed head-to-toe in the black uniform of the ninja.

We climb high into the mountains and take a short cut into the next valley. We must catch the samurai before they get to their castle.

Cho helps me across a rocky river-bed and up the other side. I'm panting now and my legs shake with the effort of the climb. As we get to the top of the ridge, Cho suddenly stops.

"We're too late," she gasps.

I look down into the gorge below where a fast-flowing river runs. Marching up the road, a troop of samurai cross the river's only bridge and enter Black Eagle Castle.

The castle rises out of the rock like the broken tooth of a giant. A high wall surrounds the castle on all sides. Samurai guards armed with spears and swords stand on the battlements.

"What do we do now?" I ask Cho.

"Wait here until sunset," she says. "Then enter the castle."

"Do you know where the Scrolls will be?"

"No," Cho replies. "But if we find Lord Oda, we find the Scrolls."

I try not to show my alarm at this plan. Back at the temple, I was confident. Now I've seen the castle, with its high walls and armed guards, I'm no longer so bold.

The sun drops behind the mountains and the gorge grows dark. In the night sky a full moon rises.

"Time to go," says Cho, running along the ridge to where a tall tree has fallen and now spans the gap.

"We'll cross one at a time. You go first," orders Cho.

I take a look at the tree she wants me to use as a bridge and an ice-cold shiver of fear runs down my spine. The river roars far below and I'm glad I can't see the terrifying drop in the darkness. As I cross, the tree creaks and groans like it's about to break.

"Keep going!" hisses Cho.

Once I get to the other side, Cho follows.

She's bolder than me and gets across in a few

easy leaps.

We now climb down the mountain side

behind the castle. It's very dangerous. The cliff

face is steep and it's hard to see where to put

my hands and feet. But we can't risk being seen by the samurai.

At last we reach the bottom and I breathe a sigh of relief.

We hide behind a rock as a samurai patrol passes by, then we make a dash for the castle wall. Cho throws her grappling hook high into the air. It catches on the top of the wall and we climb up the rope.

Then we're inside the castle and we must stay alert. Samurai are everywhere. My heart is thumping in my chest as we creep down a flight of stone stairs and into a courtyard. In the centre is a water well, on the other side a storehouse and in the far corner a cherry-blossom tree stands.

As we make our way across the courtyard, we hear the sound of footsteps. We duck inside the storehouse and watch four guards walk by.

"There are too many patrols," whispers Cho. "You stay here, while I find out where Lord Oda is."

I nod and Cho vanishes down a passageway. I want to do more than just hide but I know Cho's acrobatic skills will allow her to move through the castle without being seen. She'll find Lord Oda far quicker on her own.

As I wait for her to return, I hear voices coming from the opposite direction. Two men stride into the courtyard, with guards all round them. One is short and round as a ball.

He's talking loudly to the other, who is tall and looks like a warrior. This man is dressed in a gold silk robe with a black eagle crest on his back. In the light of a lantern, I spot the red scar on his cheek. It's Lord Oda!

Then the warlord Oda leaves the courtyard with his guards and I wonder what to do.

Should I follow?

Or should I wait for Cho?

If I wait, we might lose Lord Oda. If I go, I could find the Scrolls.

This is my chance to prove myself as a real ninja.

I stay hidden in the shadows as I follow Lord Oda to the castle's main tower. A short while later, I see lamps being lit on the third floor.

I tell myself I must remember the Grandmaster's lesson – I must come to the tower from a different direction. I climb the outside wall up to a third-floor window. When I look in, I see a painting of a black eagle on the ceiling. This must be Lord Oda's bedroom. His mattress is rolled out on the floor, ready for the night. Beside his pillow is a wooden box. A picture of two hawks is carved on the lid. Two hawks – the emblem of our clan. I've found the Scroll box!

I can hear Lord Oda and the other man talking in the next room. Without a sound, I climb in through the open window. It's very narrow, but I'm small enough to slip through. When I climb down, I land on a loose floorboard. It squeaks as my feet touch it.

In the other room the voices stop.

I've a split second to decide – I can climb back out the window ... or hide.

Lifting up the loose floorboard, I clamber into the hole below and lie down. Just as I lower the board back into place, the bedroom door slides open.

"There's no one here, my lord," says a guard, his sword at the ready. "It must have been a mouse."

"We can't be too careful now we have the Scrolls," says Lord Oda. "Double the number of patrols."

"We already have, my lord," answers the guard.

"Then double them again!" Lord Oda commands.

The guard bows and closes the door.

I decide to stay put. Now I know Lord Oda has the Scrolls, I only have to wait for him to go to bed. Then I can steal them as he sleeps. My only worry is Cho. She will think I've been caught.

By the time Lord Oda puts the Scrolls back in their box and settles down to sleep, my body is stiff from lying in the tiny space under the floorboards. I climb softly out of my hiding place and creep across the room towards the sleeping samurai. I match my breathing to his breathing, just as the Grandmaster told me.

By the pale light of the moon, I can see Lord Oda's swords lying next to his bed. It would be justice for this samurai to die by his own sword.

In my head, I hear the Grandmaster say, "Complete the mission and *nothing* else."

I have to make a choice – the Scrolls or the sword ...

As I reach out, my arm blocks the moonlight that shines onto Lord Oda's face.

A small but deadly mistake.

Lord Oda's eyes snap open. For a moment, we stare at each other in shock.

Then he screams, "GUARDS!"

I grab the box with the Scrolls and make a dash for the window. But Lord Oda grabs me before I can get there. I fight to break free, but he's too strong. As Lord Oda reaches for his sword to kill me, I thrust my thumb into the nerve point behind his collarbone.

The Dragon's Gate.

He cries out in pain and drops to the floor.

I stuff the box in my pack and scramble out the window as the guards rush into the room.

They're too big to follow me through. I clamber down the tower as fast as I can. When I am back on the ground, I run to the courtyard to find Cho. But she's nowhere to be seen.

All of a sudden, samurai guards appear from every direction and block any hope of escape.

"Kill him!" the head guard snarls.

The samurai draw their swords and attack. I take out my *shuriken*.

The pressure is on. Five throwing stars. Five samurai.

I can imagine Renzo's gloating face waiting for me to fail.

I throw one *shuriken* after the other. I hit the first samurai in the hand. He drops his sword. The second throwing star strikes the next man in the chest. The third catches the head guard in the throat. The fourth samurai is stopped by a *shuriken* blade in his arm. The fifth shuriken … misses.

It hits the cherry-blossom tree instead. The last guard swings his sword to cut my head off. It's too late for me to avoid the blade.

At the last second, Cho drops from the

tree like a black butterfly. She knocks the guard aside with a flying front kick. The tip of his sword just misses my neck.

The guard attacks Cho. As he cuts down with his sword, Cho leaps forwards and grabs his arms. She spins into him, then throws him over her shoulder. He flies through the air and falls down the well. There's a terrified scream, then a splash!

Cho turns to me. "I saw you climbing down the main tower. Did you get the Scrolls?"

I nod.

"Let's get out of here then!" she says, as more samurai pour into the courtyard.

We run up the stairs to the top of the wall. There are samurai everywhere now. A guard sees us and shouts for more men.

"Hold onto me," says Cho, and she throws

her grappling hook around a stone statue sticking out of the battlements.

The samurai close in. Cho leaps from the wall. I hang on for dear life as we swing through the air.

The ground comes rushing towards us. Cho lets go at the last second. We land, roll and jump to our feet.

Without stopping, we sprint for the bridge. There's no point climbing the cliff. We'd be shot down with arrows. Our only hope is to out-run the samurai.

But as we reach the river, we see the guards have raised the drawbridge.

"We'll have to swim," says Cho. She looks scared as she stares at the fast-flowing waters.

"The Scrolls will be ruined," I say.

"What other choice do we have?" says Cho, as the gates to Black Eagle Castle open and a mass of samurai pours out.

We look for another point to cross the river. But there's nothing. Only a few trees and a grove of tall bamboo next to the river bank.

All of a sudden I have an idea.

5. Decoy

"Where are we going?" asks Cho as I lead her into the bamboo grove. The samurai are behind us and they are getting closer.

"Up!" I reply.

Cho gives me a puzzled look.

"Trust me," I say, and I clamber up the tallest bamboo stem.

As we both reach the top, the bamboo bends under our weight. It swings down and across the river, and we fly through the air until we're hanging over the opposite bank. We both let go and drop safely to the ground.

The bamboo straightens up again as the samurai appear on the other river bank. They stare at us in shock.

"How did they get across?" shouts one of the samurai.

"They must have flown!" cries another.

"It's ninja magic," says Lord Oda. We see him walk between the samurai with his gold robe glimmering in the moonlight.

As we vanish into the darkness, he bellows, "Ninja, be warned! I'll have my revenge!"

Everyone from our village is at the temple to see us return the Scrolls.

With Cho at my side, I climb the long flight of stone steps.

"I hear you failed your black belt test ... *again*," says Renzo, as we pass him on the stairs.

"An ant never gives up," I reply. "You of all ninja should know that after five attempts."

It takes Renzo a minute to work out what I mean, but then his face goes red. His friends turn to him and it's clear they can't believe what they have just heard.

As Renzo tries to explain away his lie, Cho and I cross the courtyard to the temple. The Grandmaster is standing outside. We

kneel before him and I hand over the Scrolls.
He takes the precious box from me and puts a
black belt in my hands in its place.

"But I didn't pass your test," I say.

"The Scrolls were the test," he answers with a smile. "And you passed."

"But what if I'd failed?" I say. "Lord Oda would have all our secrets."

"I knew you wouldn't fail," the Grandmaster tells me. "This time you believed you'd pass. That is sometimes all it takes."

The Grandmaster laughs. "Anyway, they weren't the real Scrolls."

I stare at him in shock. "We risked our lives for fake Scrolls?"

The Grandmaster shakes his head. "Your mission was very important. I knew Lord Oda wanted the Scrolls. So I let him find them. However, I replaced the real ones with fakes."

"So why send us to get them back?" I ask.

"If we didn't try to steal them back, Lord Oda would guess they were fake," he explains, and I start to understand his cunning plan. "Now he thinks he knows our secrets. He thinks what he read in the Scrolls is true!"

The Grandmaster laughs again. "Lord Oda will think that a ninja can pass through walls like a ghost, transform into a spider, and even fly like a bird!"

Cho and I look at each other, and we laugh too.

"But we did!"

6. Life Force

Two months later ...

Pain rages across my chest like fire and I collapse onto the wooden floor of the temple.

An old man with a wrinkled face, pale eyes and a long grey beard stands over me. I focus and see that he is the Grandmaster. And he's just given me the Death Touch.

"The Death Touch isn't about power,"

the Grandmaster explains to the other ninja students who stand around my shaking body. "As you saw, I hardly even hit Taka."

My best friend Cho drops to her knees beside me. Her dark brown eyes are full of concern.

"What have you done to him?" Cho asks as I fight for breath.

"I've blocked his *chi*," the Grandmaster replies.

Renzo is among the students. He frowns and rubs at his shaved head in confusion. The Grandmaster is blind, but he senses the frown and turns to Renzo.

"The student who asks a question is a fool for a minute. The student who does not ask

stays a fool for ever," the Grandmaster says.

The rest of the class turn to stare at Renzo too and his face burns red with shame. All the while, I twist in agony on the floor.

After an embarrassed pause, Renzo asks, "What's ... *chi?*"

"It is your life force," the Grandmaster replies with a smile. "It's vital to your existence. You can live for three months without food. You can live for three days without water. You can live for three minutes without air. But you can't live for one second without *chi.*"

The Grandmaster holds up one bony finger to stress the single second. Then, with the same finger, he traces twelve lines across Renzo's body. "*Chi* flows through invisible energy lines in your body," he explains. "A ninja can use the Death Touch at certain points along these lines. By doing this he can block an opponent's energy. He can destroy their life force. He can even inject bad *chi* into them."

As the Death Touch squeezes the life out of me, the Grandmaster's voice becomes distant in my ears. It's as if he's speaking from the back of a cave. The pain spreads to my arms and legs and I can no longer move.

Cho sees the terror in my eyes. "I think Taka's had enough –" she begins.

Renzo interrupts her. "Is Taka dying?"

"If I don't unblock his *chi*, yes he will die," the Grandmaster replies.

Renzo looks down at me and grins.

"Oh dear, that would be a pity," he says. It's

obvious he's not upset by the idea at all.

I start to panic. I'm fourteen years old, too young to die. My chest now feels as if it's being crushed by a huge rock and I can't breathe.

But the Grandmaster doesn't try to save me.

He just goes on with his lesson. "If you're an expert and know which points on the human body to strike, it's very easy to kill someone with the Death Touch," he explains. "The real skill lies in *not* killing the person."

"So when do *we* learn the Death Touch?" Renzo asks. He flexes his fingers, keen to begin.

The Grandmaster gives Renzo a stern look. "You must learn to walk before you can run," he replies. "First, I'll teach you the points that will stop your enemy's sword arm. But that will be tomorrow's lesson."

The Grandmaster reaches for his wooden staff and hobbles away.

"Grandmaster!" Cho calls. "What about Taka?"

The Grandmaster stops and turns back with a surprised look on his face. "Sorry, I almost forgot. Old age must be catching up on me," he explains. "Help Taka to stand."

Cho and two other students pick me up. I hang like a broken puppet in their arms.

The Grandmaster presses three nerve points in my back. In an instant the pain disappears. I feel like I've been reborn.

"Are you all right?" Cho asks as I sway on my wobbly legs.

"I am now," I gasp. I hold a hand to my thumping heart. "But remind me never to volunteer to help the Grandmaster show a new move again!"

I drive my spade into the muddy ditch then heave a mound of earth onto the steep bank above me. I try to ignore the aches and pains in my body. After a month of Death Touch training, every student is battered and bruised. It takes a lot of practice to target the correct points on the *chi* lines and most of the time we get it wrong!

"My back is killing me," moans Jun, a tall

thin boy who is working in another ditch. He stands up and stretches and then calls out to the teacher who is watching us work. "Sensei, the rice fields are already dug. What's the point of all these extra ditches and banks?"

Sensei Shima gives him a hard stare. "A ninja must hear what is silent, see what is invisible and bear what is painful," he says. "If you cannot see what you're doing here, then you need to dig a little longer."

The students in the class all look at one another. The purpose of the ditches is still a mystery to us. Sensei Shima normally teaches us combat and battle tactics, but for the last few weeks we've spent most of our time chopping wood, building fences and digging ditches.

71

"I expect these ditches to be finished by sunset," Sensei Shima tells us. Then he strides off towards his farmhouse and disappears inside.

"I don't believe it!" Renzo yells. He throws down his spade in disgust. "Sensei Shima goes off to drink tea, while we slave away in the dirt!"

Renzo's friend Yoko wipes mud from her face and grumbles. "Last lesson we were tying back tree branches for him," she says. "Before that he made us carry firewood onto the mountain ridges and out into the fields. None of this makes any sense. We're supposed to be ninja, not gardeners!"

"Too right," Renzo agrees. "When are we going to do something worth doing? The

Grandmaster's Death Touch lessons are so much more fun."

He closes his fingers to form a snakehead fist. This is the lethal strike that the Grandmaster has just taught us earlier that morning.

"This lesson is worth doing," says Cho, who has already dug half of her ditch. "It keeps us fit and strong so that we can climb walls, jump high and speed-run."

"But I'm already strong," Renzo argues. He flexes the impressive muscles in his arms and then turns to me. "Taka, you dig my trench."

"Why me?" I protest.

"Because your puny body needs the exercise," he says with a laugh.

Renzo is my rival and so he always picks on me. But now I have completed my first mission and I am a black belt, I'm no longer scared of him.

"Sensei Shima says a ninja doesn't have to be strong," I reply. "In fact, the best ninja are lean and quick – not fat and slow."

Renzo leaps into my ditch and squares up to me.

"That's fighting talk," he growls. "You think you're a hero just because you saved the ninja Scrolls, don't you? Well, you're not. I heard your father was killed running away from the

Battle of Black Eagle. He was a coward – and that means you must be too."

Renzo's insult to my dead father makes me explode with anger. I raise my spade to knock him over. In the blink of an eye, Renzo makes his snakehead fist and strikes a nerve point in my shoulder. My arm goes limp and I drop my spade.

"Too weak to hold the spade, are we?" Renzo smirks.

No matter how hard I try, I can't move my arm. It's gone totally numb and hangs limp by my side.

"Unlock my arm!" I demand.

Renzo shrugs in a fake apology. "Sorry, but I haven't learned how to release it yet."

"Then I'll do it," says Cho. She jumps into the ditch and inspects my arm.

"Poor Taka," Renzo mocks. "He needs a girl to rescue him."

"Go and bash your head against a temple bell," Cho snaps, as she tries to find the correct point to release my arm. But after three attempts it stays locked.

"I don't know what Renzo's done to you," she sighs. "You'll have to visit the Grandmaster."

With Cho's help, I climb out of the ditch. The Grandmaster's temple is high on the ridge to the north of us and I stagger towards the long path that winds up the mountain. I glare at Renzo as I leave.

"You'd better hurry." Renzo laughs and points to the sun, which is sinking low in the sky. "You still have your ditch to finish."

7. Fatal Message

"Renzo has certainly mastered that skill," the Grandmaster says. He seems both impressed at his student's skill and disappointed with the fact he has used it on me. "But he has yet to master himself," he tells me.

"I know," I reply, as I flex my arm and shake the stiffness from it. "Renzo always wants to prove he's better than me."

"Then that's his problem," the

Grandmaster says. "It's more important to be the best that you can be than to worry about being better than someone else."

He lays a kind hand on my arm.

"Next time, try not to let your anger control you," he advises me. "Anger is like a hot coal. When you grasp it to throw it at someone else, it burns you instead."

He picks up his staff and leaves me in the garden to think about his words of wisdom.

I head back down through the forest. Now it's autumn, all the leaves are turning gold, orange and red.

Through a gap in the trees, I spy our village far below. It is hidden deep in a remote valley and can only be reached by a few steep mountain passes. The route is our clan's best-kept secret.

I kick at a pile of fallen leaves as I wander along the path. Despite the Grandmaster's advice, I'm still furious at what Renzo said about my father. I know so little about him. He was killed by the samurai Lord Oda when I was only a baby.

Was he really a coward?

Further along the path I'm surprised to spot my mother. Then I see she's cutting a puffball mushroom from the base of a tree. Everyone in the village visits her for her powerful herbal medicines and I know that she uses mushroom spores to cure infected wounds.

She looks up in joy. "Taka! What are you doing up here?"

"I had to see the Grandmaster," I explain.

My mother smiles proudly.

I realise she has a secret hope that he's preparing me to be the next Grandmaster. I decide not to tell her the real reason for my visit. But I do have to ask one very important question.

"Mother," I say. "Did my father die running *away* from the Battle of Black Eagle?"

Her smile vanishes and she looks shocked. "Who told you that?"

"Renzo," I admit.

My mother scowls. "That boy is a pest. Listen, Taka. Your father was a true warrior."

"But *who* was he? You never talk about him."

My mother sighs. "It's difficult to explain. You see –"

All of a sudden she stops talking. Behind us we hear footsteps crunch through the forest. We glance at each other, worried.

No ninja would make that much noise.

I disappear into a bush beside the path. My mother hides behind a tree.

Even though we're close to our own village, a ninja must always be on guard. Our clan leader Tenshin has warned us about an increase in samurai patrols. Lord Oda has vowed to destroy every ninja clan in his domain. Even since I stole back our clan's

Scrolls from him four months ago, he's been hunting the mountains for us.

The crunch of leaves gets closer. The footsteps are heavy and uneven. I can now hear breathing, harsh and rapid.

If the intruder is a samurai, we have to kill him. We can't let him escape to tell Lord Oda where our village is.

My mother pulls out her knife.

I reach into my belt and select three *shuriken*. These ninja stars are fast, silent and tipped with deadly poison. They're my weapon of choice.

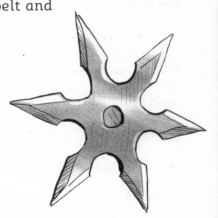

The bushes ahead begin to rustle. I get ready to throw my *shuriken*.

A man staggers onto the forest path. He's dressed in robes the colour of saffron. He carries a trumpet made from a conch shell and he leans on a wooden staff. He appears to be a *yamabushi*, a mountain monk.

The monk falls against a tree and I spot two arrows sticking out of his back.

"Riku!" my mother cries. She darts out from her hiding place.

I look again. He's in disguise, but now I recognise the man's face. He's one of Tenshin's best spies.

Riku collapses into my mother's arms. She lowers him to the ground, opens her medicine bag and starts to tend the arrow wounds.

"No, Akemi ..." Riku groans. "You must ... listen first ..."

Riku's breathing is shallow and his voice is weak. We both lean closer to hear his words.

"I was spying in Black Eagle Castle ... I

heard Lord Oda ... I don't know how ... but he's found out where our village is!"

My mother and I look at one another in shock.

"Then we must close the mountain passes," my mother says.

'Too late," says Riku, as he gasps his last, dying breath. "Lord Oda ... is on the march ... with his army. They'll be here by sunrise."

8. Invisible Defences

I join Cho in the village square just before dawn. Like me, she's wearing her black *gi*. Our ninja uniform has our emblem of two hawks on the front.

We take our place among the rest of the clan. Every ninja is dressed for battle and carries a weapon. Cho is armed with her double-edged sword. Jun has a pair of *kama* – curved blades with wooden shafts. Renzo

twirls his *nunchaku* – two sticks joined by a chain. Of course, he is showing off to Yoko who is wearing her *shuko* – cat claws. My belt is packed with *shuriken*.

Renzo glances over at me. "Didn't expect to see that coward here!" he says to Yoko.

I feel my anger rise.

Cho grabs my arm to stop me. "He's not
your enemy today!" she tells me. "Lord Oda is."

I try to control my temper. "I know," I
say. "But we should all be on the same side!"

Our clan leader climbs the village watch
tower with Sensei Shima. He holds up his hand
to get us to listen.

"All ninja know that the greatest victory is the battle not fought," he declares. "But in this case, Lord Oda has left us with no choice. We must defend our homes. But do not fear, for Sensei Shima and I have been planning for just such an attack."

He nods at Sensei Shima, who orders two men to divert the stream that runs through our village. They open a floodgate and the ditches we dug fill up in minutes. I gasp with surprise as a large ring of water surrounds us. Cho and the other ninja students stare in equal amazement. Sensei Shima has built a moat around the village.

His words come back to me. A ninja must ... *see what is invisible.*

At last I can see all the defences that we've been working on this past month.

* The high banks of earth we built are really a maze of walls to protect us from an enemy army.

* The paths between the paddy fields are so narrow that only one person at a time can pass along them.

* The bamboo fences we made form a spiked barrier around the village square.

* The tree branches that we tied back at the edge of the forest are booby traps. The trip-wires are hidden in the bushes.

We didn't realise at the time, but we were turning the village into a fortress!

On the ridge to the east, a spiral of smoke rises into the dawn sky. It's a warning signal from one of our ninja scouts.

"Lord Oda is here!" Tenshin announces. His face is grave. "Let us welcome him and his army in true ninja style."

Then he grins and raises his famous Sword of Destruction. The lethal edge of the blade is jagged like a saw.

The clan all raise their weapons in salute and we shout a mighty battle cry.

The roar of our voices makes me feel strong and brave.

Then we fall silent as a gold flag with the crest of a black eagle appears on the ridge. Then another. And another ...

Soon the whole mountain ridge is lined with flags. They flap in the wind like a flock of vultures.

In spite of the bravery I felt during the battle cry, the sight of so many warriors sends an icy cold shiver down my spine.

Lord Oda has brought an army of over one thousand samurai.

Against a village of fewer than one hundred ninja.

What chance do we have?

"Lord Oda demands your surrender," the samurai messenger states. Having ridden his horse down the valley, he waits at the border of our village for our reply.

Tenshin laughs at the idea, then shouts back. "Tell Lord Oda that we demand *his* surrender."

The samurai is stunned by Tenshin's answer. "B ... but there are ten of us to every one of you!"

"Yes," Tenshin agrees cheerfully. "It's a shame you didn't bring more men. Your defeat will be swift and shameful."

The samurai is unable to believe his ears. He pulls on his horse's reins and gallops back up the valley to tell Lord Oda.

I am shocked too. "Does Tenshin really think we can win?" I whisper to Cho.

"Think?" answers the Grandmaster, who appears behind me. "He *knows* we can."

"But their army is sure to beat us," Cho says. Her eyes scan the rows upon rows of swords, spears and battle axes.

The Grandmaster leans on his staff and taps a finger to his head. "A winner wins in his mind first, then goes to war. A loser goes to war and then seeks to win. Tenshin has already won the battle in his head. That's what you both need to do now."

I follow the Grandmaster's advice and try to imagine our victory, but the thought of the bloody conflict terrifies me.

The Grandmaster lays a hand on my arm and studies me with his blind eyes. "Are you scared, Taka?"

I realise there's no point in lying to the Grandmaster. He may be blind, but he always sees the truth. I hope Renzo can't hear my reply as I admit, "Yes."

"Good. You should be," says the Grandmaster, to my surprise. "Fear can make a mouse attack a lion. Use your fear to give you strength. Remember the skills I've taught you and you will live to see another day."

With that, he hobbles away to offer a

boost to the other young ninja who face their first battle.

"Don't worry," says Cho. "I'll protect your back."

I offer a smile in return. "And I'll protect yours."

As we bump fists in a bond of friendship, an angry cry echoes through the valley. I look up and see that the samurai messenger has delivered our clan leader's reply to Lord Oda.

Lord Oda roars down at us from high on the ridge. "PREPARE TO DIE, NINJA!"

97

9. Death Touch

Lord Oda and his army thunder down the mountain like a tidal wave.

I grab my *shuriken*, but fear fills my heart and my hand begins to tremble. Then I look at Cho and remember the Grandmaster's words. I feel a surge of strength.

I am a ninja and I'll protect my family, friends and clan with my life if I have to.

As the first line of samurai advances

into the trees, their horses' hooves trigger the hidden trip-wires. Long branches whip back and knock the samurai from their saddles. The charge turns into chaos as the horses run off in different directions without their riders.

But a second wave of samurai are not far behind. There are no tree traps left now, so they reach the valley bottom unharmed. Tenshin orders a group of ninja to let loose a volley of flaming arrows from their bows.

The arrows shoot through the air ... but miss every single samurai!

I groan in despair before I realise that the samurai weren't the target – the wood piles we stacked in the fields are. The piles are soaked in lamp oil and gunpowder and they

explode into lethal firebombs that engulf the enemy in flames.

Our clan lets out a huge cheer as the samurai advance is stopped in its tracks.

"We're going to win this battle!" I shout, and I punch the air in victory.

"It's not over yet," Cho warns.

She points to where Lord Oda is rallying his forces to launch a fresh assault. A new troop of samurai avoids the flaming wood piles and charges down the only road into our village. The route has been left open to attack and I fear our defences have failed.

But then the whole troop disappears.

We hear their moans and cries of pain. The troop ran straight into a deep trench covered with a mesh of sticks and autumn leaves. The trench is filled with sharp stones and bamboo spikes. The samurai had no idea it was there until they hit the stones and spikes!

Lord Oda goes into a rage when he realises he has lost over a third of his men already.

"I'LL MAKE YOU SUFFER FOR YOUR NINJA TRICKS!" he screams.

Lord Oda directs what is left of his army to head to the south. He leads the charge across the moat himself. The deep water slows their horses and the ninja with bows shoot arrow after arrow, picking off as many samurai as they can.

But the moat can't stop an entire army. Soon the samurai are clambering onto the banks and storming the village.

The battle between ninja and samurai now truly begins.

"ATTACK!" Tenshin shouts as he rushes forward to engage with the enemy. His Sword

of Destruction cuts through the ranks of samurai like they were origami soldiers.

Sensei Shima is right behind Tenshin. His sword is a blur as he and the other clan members fight to defend our village.

Renzo is the first of the young ninja to do battle. His spinning *nunchaku* knocks out samurai after samurai. As much as I dislike Renzo, I have to admire his bravery. The rest of the ninja are inspired by his courage. They raise their weapons and charge forward.

I stand back-to-back with Cho as Lord Oda's army surges across the rice fields and into the village. Cho's double-edged sword means she's always on the attack, no matter which way she swings her weapon.

A samurai leaps at me and Cho stops him dead before he gets anywhere near.

"Thanks!" I gasp. "I owe you one."

Two samurai rush at Cho. I double-throw two *shuriken*. The ninja stars hit both samurai in the throat.

"Now I owe you," Cho says as her two attackers fall to the ground, with blood pouring from their wounds.

Then I spot a samurai with a barbed spear rush at the Grandmaster.

"Watch out!" I cry, even though I know the Grandmaster can't see him.

But the Grandmaster is already aware of the danger. He flicks the end of his staff towards the charging samurai. The hollow end of the staff sends a poison dart into the man's neck. The samurai drops to the ground, dead.

Another samurai slices downwards with his sword. The Grandmaster hits him in the shoulder with his staff. As the samurai drops his weapon, the Grandmaster strikes with a snakehead fist just below the man's heart. The samurai collapses – a victim of the Death Touch.

More samurai attack the blind Grandmaster. Each suffers a similar fate. Soon there's a pile of bodies knee-deep around him.

I realise the Grandmaster can look after himself and concentrate on fighting my own battles. The village is now swarming with samurai and our clan is in danger of being overcome.

I throw *shuriken* after *shuriken*, and take down as many of the enemy as I can. But then I reach into my belt and discover I've only got one ninja star left. And there are still hundreds of samurai ...

I hear a cry for help. To my right, a samurai with a huge battle axe cuts through the chain of Renzo's *nunchaku* and kicks him to the ground. Renzo has no way to defend himself. He is about to be chopped in half.

Without a second thought, I throw my last *shuriken* to save my rival. The ninja star strikes the samurai in the arm and he loses his grip on his axe. But the poison is slow to act and the samurai draws his sword to kill Renzo.

I rush forward and launch myself into a flying kick. My foot smashes into the samurai's chest. He staggers backwards, trips over a body and ends up skewered on the spiked bamboo fence.

Renzo stares up at me in shock.

"No need to thank me," I say, as I hurry off to find Cho again.

But Renzo leaps to his feet and calls after me. "I was wrong," he shouts. "You're no coward."

Then he looks past me and narrows his eyes in fury. "But Cho is."

As I turn, I see my friend flee the battle and escape up the mountain.

10. Deadly Mission

I can't believe Cho would run away. We'd sworn to protect each other. But when I look around the village, I realise our defeat is inevitable.

The sheer size of Lord Oda's army is too great. Half of my clan are already dead or dying.

Tenshin calls for any ninja still alive to retreat to the village square.

I run with Renzo for this last stronghold. A samurai is right behind us, slashing with his sword. We turn into an alley and leap over a hidden ditch. The samurai follows but he doesn't see the ditch. We hear his screams as he tumbles into the trap.

Renzo and I are the last ninja to make it into the village square. Tenshin and Sensei Shima rush to close the gate in the spiked fence.

I spot my mother among the survivors and breathe a sigh of relief. We are safe ... but only for the moment.

Lord Oda and his army surround us on all sides. The samurai begin to burn our farmhouses to the ground. I even see a fire blazing in the Grandmaster's temple high on the ridge. Lord Oda is destroying everything.

"You should have surrendered while you had the chance," Lord Oda yells to us. "Now you will all die."

He orders his men to attack. They chop at the spiked bamboo fence with their axes. Tenshin and the other ninja do their best to fend them off. But the samurai are unstoppable. They break through into the square.

Sensei Shima is cut down in an instant. Jun is swamped by five samurai at once and doesn't get up again. Yoko fights as fiercely as a tiger but is soon wounded. Renzo snatches up a broken spear and races to her defence.

I have no more *shuriken*. When a samurai charges at me, I can only fling mud into his eyes. As soon as he is blinded, I front-kick him in the gut and knock him out with a hammer-fist strike to the top of the head.

Then I see the Grandmaster, battling three samurai on his own with his staff snapped in half. As I fight my way to him, I come face-to-face with Lord Oda.

He glares at me.

"I recognise your eyes, ninja!" he snarls. "You're the one who stole back the Scrolls."

"And I recognise your ugly red scar!" I reply in insult.

I look to my left and spy someone's sword on the ground.

If I can kill Lord Oda, then the battle would be over – like cutting the head off a snake!

Lord Oda sees me glance at the weapon and grins. "Do you think you can get to it in time?" he taunts.

I realise this is my chance to avenge my murdered father. I dive for the sword. Lord Oda lunges to cut me in half … but my move was a fake.

As Lord Oda attacks the wrong way, he exposes his chest. I switch direction, dart forwards and strike him with a snakehead fist in the heart.

Death Touch!

But Lord Oda doesn't die. He just laughs at me.

"Your ninja magic won't work on me!"
Lord Oda says.

I stare in shock at the samurai lord.
I know that I hit the exact nerve point the
Grandmaster taught me. There is no way Lord
Oda should have survived my attack. Was he
immortal? Or had I got the Death Touch wrong?

Lord Oda sees the painful confusion in my face.

"I was born to survive," he reveals with a grin. "My heart is on the opposite side."

He taps the right side of his chest. Now I understand why the Death Touch didn't work – the strike points are reversed.

"I told you I'd have my revenge," Lord Oda gloats and he thrusts with his sword.

"NO! Not my son!" my mother cries. She leaps to save me.

My mother lands between us and Lord Oda's sword goes straight through her instead of me.

"Mother!" I cry as she collapses in my arms, blood pouring from her stomach. I clasp

her to me to try to stop the bleeding. "Please
don't die," I beg.

"Taka ... don't cry," she groans.
"Sometimes ... a price must be paid ... to
protect those you love ..."

Her eyes close and her body goes limp in my arms.

"NO!" I scream.

Lord Oda stands over me, staring at my mother's dead body.

Through my tears of grief, I look to the sky and see dark red autumn leaves fall like drops of blood into the valley.

Then I see a river of black flowing down the mountain. I have to wipe away my tears before I realise that it's another ninja clan. Cho is leading them. I can see her double-edged sword glinting in the morning sun.

A samurai officer rushes over to Lord Oda.

"We must retreat, Lord Oda!" he insists,

with a fearful glance at the new ninja clan.

But Lord Oda doesn't move. His bodyguards have to drag him away as the ninja clan storms into the village and begins to wipe out his army. The rest of the samurai drop their weapons and flee for their lives.

As the last of them disappear over the ridge, a huge cheer of victory fills the valley.

Against all the odds, the ninja have won.

I pack my belt with as many *shuriken* as I can find. Then I fill another bag with rope, *shuko* climbing claws, a knife, my mother's herbal medicine, a flint and steel for making fire, food, a water skin and spare clothes.

Before I head out the door, I take one last

look around the wreck of my house. My bed is ripped to shreds. The kitchen is smashed to pieces. And the hearth, where a fire always used to burn, is cold and empty. Now my mother is dead, the place no longer feels like home.

There's a knock at the door. It's Cho – the star of the battle. She had the good sense to light the distress beacon in the Grandmaster's temple and summon another ninja clan to our aid.

"Are you ready to go?" Cho asks me.

We may have won the battle, but Tenshin has decided that the clan must move deeper into the mountains and find a new hidden valley.

"I'm not going with the clan," I reply.

Cho's eyes widen in surprise.

"I have to find Lord Oda."

"What?" she cries.

"If someone doesn't stop him, he'll only return with a bigger army, hunt us down and destroy our clan for ever," I explain. "I plan to cut the head off the snake."

Cho looks at me as if I'm mad. "Have you told the Grandmaster about this?"

I shake my head.

"But a mission like that is a death wish," she argues. "With all the bodyguards he has, you'll never get close enough to him."

"I've been close twice before," I reply. "I can do it again."

"Not on your own," she says. "I'll come with you."

"No," I say, although I'm touched by her loyalty. "It's too great a risk."

Cho gives me a hard stare. "We made a battle-bond," she reminds me. "You protect my back, I protect yours. As this battle isn't over, our bond isn't either."

I smile at her. "You're a true friend," I say. I realise my chances of success are far greater with Cho by my side.

Just as we're about to leave, Renzo appears. "I overheard your plan. I want to come too."

"Why?" I ask. I am suspicious of his motives.

Renzo bows his head in remorse. "I owe you my life," he explains. "As a ninja brother, it's my duty to help you any way I can."

I turn to Cho for her opinion. She just shrugs. "He could carry all our bags."

Although Renzo is my rival, I respect his strength and courage. "You realise there may be no going back?" I say.

Renzo grins. "I like a challenge!"

The decision made, we all bump fists in a battle-bond. Then we slip silently into the night.

Three ninja on a deadly mission ...

11. Snow Patrol

I climb the steep mountain path with Cho
and Renzo.

We're almost at the top of the ridge, near
our village temple, when a voice speaks from
the darkness. "Where are you three going?" it
demands.

We spin round to see the Grandmaster
of our ninja clan. He glares at us with eyes
as pale as the moon. He is old and blind, but

his other senses are sharp enough to 'see' the world around him.

I know that he could tell if I lied, and so I reply with the truth.

"Black Eagle Castle."

"I suppose you intend to kill Lord Oda?" the Grandmaster says. There is disapproval in his voice.

My silence is all the answer he needs.

"I expect you haven't told Tenshin," the Grandmaster goes on. "Our clan leader would not agree to such a mission."

"But Lord Oda has attacked our village and killed half our clan!" I protest. "Surely, he deserves to die?"

By way of reply, the Grandmaster points

to the graveyard beside the temple. Four rows of new graves mark the ninja who were lost in the battle the day before. A shovel still sticks out of a pile of earth.

The Grandmaster speaks in a solemn tone. "A wise man once said, before you embark on a journey of revenge, dig two graves," he says. "One for your enemy and one for yourself."

"But we won't fail," I reply. I sound more confident than I really feel.

The Grandmaster gives a sorry shake of his head. "You misunderstand, Taka. Revenge cannot heal the hurts of the heart any more than salt water can quench thirst."

"But Lord Oda murdered my father ... and now my mother too," I cry. "I want justice!"

"Your mother Akemi protected you so that you could live on," the Grandmaster says. "She was a healer. She wouldn't want you to risk your life in a hunt for revenge."

"But I'm a ninja," I remind him. "You

made me a black belt, you even showed me the Death Touch. Why teach me those skills if you don't want me to be an assassin?"

"I'm teaching you how to be a spy and defend yourself, not to be a cold-blooded killer," is the Grandmaster's stern reply. He looks at each of us in turn. "None of you has completed your training – you know so little of the world beyond this valley."

"That may be true, but together we're stronger than one ninja alone," says Renzo. He clasps me and Cho with his meaty arms.

"And we made a battle-bond," Cho explains. She clenches her fist and bumps it against mine.

The Grandmaster sighs. "I suppose that in order to see the light you must risk the

dark. And I sense that I can't persuade you from this path. I also accept that a battle-bond cannot be broken. Wait here."

The Grandmaster limps off into the temple, and it is clear that the wounds from yesterday's battle are still raw. He returns with a small pouch, a short length of bamboo and a chain with heavy weights at each end.

"Cho, this is for you," says the Grandmaster. He hands her the bamboo and some feathered darts. "Your name means 'butterfly', but this will help you sting like a bee."

"A blowpipe." Cho grins as she inspects the hollow bamboo tube.

"It's not a toy!" the Grandmaster warns her. "Be very careful with the darts. They're tipped with poison that will knock a man out."

Cho bows her thanks. Then she slips the blowpipe and darts into her backpack, beside her double-edged sword.

The Grandmaster presents Renzo with the weighted chain. "This *manriki* weapon is made of steel and is strong like you," he says. "Use it to protect your friends."

"A Ten Thousand Power Chain!" Renzo exclaims. He whips one end of the chain through the air. It whizzes like a mad wasp. "I've always wanted one of these."

The Grandmaster turns to me. "Since you're blind to my wisdom, Taka, I give you this to disable your enemy in a fight."

"Thank you," I reply with respect. I take the pouch of fine-ground blinding powder and attach it to my belt.

"Do not think these weapons mean that I bless your mission," the Grandmaster says. "You will need more than luck to succeed."

For a moment, his words make me question my decision to hunt Lord Oda. But then I think of my mother dying in battle under that samurai's sword and I realise I've no choice in the matter.

I bow farewell to the Grandmaster, then I head up the mountain path with Cho and Renzo.

Before we disappear over the top, the Grandmaster calls after us. "I'll wait for you here and pray for your safe return. Remember our clan's motto –

When you hide, stay still as a shadow.

When you appear, strike like lightning!"

Three months later ...

I peer over a mound of snow. Between a gap in the trees, I spy Lord Oda.

This man, with the red scar across his cheek, is my mortal enemy.

Lord Oda sits huddled in thick blankets in a sedan chair carried by four porters. The porters struggle with their heavy burden as they hurry down the road to the gate of Black Eagle Castle. The winter sun is setting over the mountains and the porters look nervous, in spite of the samurai soldiers that protect them.

Lord Oda's bodyguards are at the front

of the line – ten warriors with the crest of a black eagle on their chests. A troop of heavily armed samurai in blood-red armour follows close behind. They wear a different crest – a roaring tiger's head. This is the emblem of Lord Kujo, the Regent of Japan.

I did not expect these samurai and their presence here is worrying. But all I care about is that Lord Oda has at last returned home to

his fortress, Black Eagle Castle. After three long months of waiting, the time has come to avenge my murdered parents.

Just as I'm about to make my move, I hear voices.

"It's so cold my eyelids are freezing together!" the first voice says.

"Stop complaining, Genzo," another man growls.

I look to my right and see a patrol of four samurai marching through the forest. I'm wearing my all-white *gi*, the ninja uniform used for winter missions, so the patrol hasn't spotted me yet ... but they are headed my way.

"Why do we have to patrol so far out from the castle?" asks the one called Genzo.

He is a stick-thin man, and he hugs himself for warmth.

The leader is shivering too, but he ignores the cold as he replies. "Now our lord is back, his adviser Kenji fears a revenge attack by the ninja. So we must be on high alert. Spread out!"

The patrol splits up. Genzo passes around a snowy rock and now he is only a few feet away from me. If he keeps coming, I'm sure to be discovered.

I reach into my bag and pull out a *shuriken*. I'm careful to hide the throwing star's gleam from the eyes of the approaching samurai.

A pine cone drops in the snow beside my face.

I glance up. Cho is in the tree above me. Her long black hair is tucked inside her white hood and she's invisible among the snowy branches. Cho notices the *shuriken* in my hand and shakes her head at me.

Don't attack, she warns me with a glare.

But Genzo is so close I can see the dirt under his toenails. One more step and he'll be standing right on top of me.

I grip my *shuriken*, ready to leap up. I will let nothing stop me in my mission.

12. Invisible

The samurai Genzo stops on the mound of snow and looks around the silent forest.

As I prepare to leap up, I recall the Grandmaster's words from three months ago – *When you appear, strike like lightning ...*

"We're wasting our time," Genzo grumbles. "There's no one out here."

The patrol leader stomps his feet to keep warm as he scans the empty landscape again.

"You're right," he says. "And it'll be dark soon. Any ninja crazy enough to be out here will freeze to death by morning."

The patrol turns back and heads towards the castle.

When I'm certain the samurai are gone, I rise up from behind the mound. Cho drops down from her hiding place in the tree.

"What were you thinking?" she whispers. "If you'd attacked that samurai, we would have had to kill them all. And a missing patrol would alert Lord Oda to the fact that we are here."

I know Cho is right. But after waiting so long for my enemy to return home, I'm impatient to get on with the mission.

"He was getting too close," I say, by way of an excuse.

"You can say that again," a rock a few feet away agrees. "He walked right past me."

Renzo uncurls himself and snow tumbles off his broad back as he loses his boulder shape.

One of the secret arts of the ninja is to be invisible. As the Grandmaster once explained, this isn't the same as disappearing. It means learning how to hide in plain sight. You can climb a tree, since people rarely look up. Or stand in a field like a scarecrow. You can disguise yourself as a samurai, a monk or even a geisha girl. You can use camouflage to blend into the surroundings or change your body shape as Renzo had.

"That samurai wouldn't have spotted a pink-bottomed monkey in a kimono!" says Cho. "He was cold and wanted to get back to a warm fire."

"Well, no harm's been done," Renzo says, as he gives me a friendly slap on the back. "Not yet anyway," he adds, with a look in the direction of Lord Oda's castle.

I know Renzo is being friendly, but ... I can't quite forget that he used to be my arch enemy among the clan. Cho wasn't happy when he volunteered to join us on our mission. She doesn't trust him ... and I suppose I shouldn't either.

"Let's make a move," Cho says. "We need to be in position before night falls."

We head to the cliff that overlooks Black Eagle Castle. This was the route Cho and I took the first time we sneaked into the fortress to steal back the Scrolls.

But there is a problem.

Now that Lord Oda has returned, there are double the number of sentries around the castle, and samurai are stationed at the base of the cliff.

"Should we wait a few more days until they relax their guard?" Cho suggests.

"No," says Renzo. "We should enter while they're still settling down."

Cho shoots him an annoyed look. "But

our plan didn't take account of the Regent's samurai that came in with Lord Oda!"

"All the more reason to go in now before they learn the layout of the castle," Renzo answers back.

Cho is about to reply, but I hold up my hand to stop them arguing. For the past three months, they've disagreed on everything, from tactics to weapons to food.

"Both of you are right," I tell them. "But we've waited long enough. We kill Lord Oda *tonight*."

We hide in the tree-line while we wait for yet another samurai patrol to pass. Because of the guards at the bottom of the cliff, we've had to change our plan and make our approach along the gorge. The route is risky, since it's so open, and we must cross the river. But we've no other option.

Before we leave the forest, we attach wooden soles to our *tabi* boots.

"Ready?" I ask.

Cho and Renzo nod.

As soon as the patrol is out of sight, we sprint across open ground.

I snatch a look back at our footprints in the snow. No samurai will ever know that we've passed this way. During our months of waiting for Lord Oda to return home, Cho carved three pairs of *ashiaro*, wooden animal footprints.

With these on our feet, all we leave behind
are the tracks of a fox, a deer and a dog.

The freezing night air chills my lungs
as we run to the edge of the gorge. In the
distance I can just see the sentries in the
castle watchtowers. But the moonless night
and our white *gi* make it impossible to spot us
against the snow.

We reach the gorge unseen. The drawbridge has been raised. But we expected that. We take off the *ashiaro* and clamber down the rock face to the river below.

The stone is cold and slippery. My fingers become numb within seconds. I hold on as tight as I can. But one false move and I'll plummet to the rocks far below.

At last my feet touch down on the river bank and I let out a sigh of relief.

At the bottom, we discover that luck is on our side. The river has iced over.

I throw a stone onto the crisp white surface of the ice. The stone bounces and skitters. Next I test its strength with my weight. The ice holds and appears to be solid ... near the bank, at least.

Cho offers to go first. She skims across with no problems.

I follow, sliding my feet so as to keep my balance. As I reach the middle of the river, the ice creaks and groans beneath me. A tiny crack appears in its surface. I slide faster, praying that I'll get across in time.

With a final burst of speed, I reach the other side.

Now it's Renzo's turn. He places a foot on the ice. Then another. With nervous steps he begins his crossing. All is going well until we hear a loud CRACK!

Renzo's eyes widen in alarm. The cracks spread through the ice like a spider's web. He starts to run. Cho and I wave our arms to urge him on.

Renzo's foot goes through the ice. He falls, but he manages to launch himself forward. He slides the last few feet to the bank and beaches himself like a sea lion.

"Full marks for style." Cho smirks.

Renzo glares up at her, then shakes his

wet foot. "Taka weakened the ice, that's all," he grumbles.

"Let's hope no one heard the ice break," I say.

I scan the top of the gorge for samurai. When no patrol appears, we climb up the other side.

At the top we put on our *ashiaro* again and make a final dash to the castle wall.

So far, so good.

We stay in the shadows as we creep along the base to our chosen entry point. The gates are heavily guarded and the battlements are crawling with samurai, but last month Cho spotted a row of stone-dropping holes in the eastern tower.

"There's our way in," she whispers. She points above our heads. "The holes are blocked by hatches, but we can cut our way through –"

All of a sudden, Renzo grabs Cho's arm and pulls her backwards. "Watch out!" he hisses.

Cho and I look down. The vicious teeth of a steel mantrap peek out from the snow's surface.

Cho shrugs Renzo off. "Don't worry, I saw it," she replies, as she steps around the deadly trap.

But this is a terrible mistake. Her foot triggers a second hidden trap.

The steel jaws of the trap clamp shut on Cho's leg. Her eyes flare wide in shock and terror. But she doesn't scream. She just bites hard on her hand, and lets out the softest of whimpers. Even in her agony, she knows that any cry could alert the sentries.

I drop to my knees and try to pull the trap apart. But the jaws won't budge. Blood is gushing from the wound where the teeth have bitten into Cho's flesh.

Renzo grabs hold of the mantrap too. He grits his teeth and pulls at the jaws. But the spring is strong. Renzo's arms are like knotted ropes, but even he can't open the trap wide enough to get Cho's leg out.

Cho is close to passing out with pain.

Renzo strains his muscles as he makes one last superhuman effort to free her. The jaws part a little ... then a little more.

As soon as the jagged teeth are clear of Cho's flesh, I pull her leg out. Renzo lets go and the jaws snap shut again like the bite of a hungry shark.

Cho lies in the snow. "Th ... thank you ... Renzo," she moans.

"No problem," Renzo replies, "but you owe me one."

I grab my mother's medicine kit from my pack and smother Cho's cuts in a thick green paste.

"This will stop the bleeding and numb the pain," I explain.

Cho nods as I wrap her leg in a white bandage.

Renzo scans for patrols. "We should abort the mission," he says.

"No!" Cho gasps. "We can't turn back now."

"But you're hurt," I say. "I'm not leaving you here."

"And I'm not carrying you," Renzo grunts.

"You don't need to!" Cho replies. She struggles to her feet and tests her leg. "Look, Akemi's medicine is already working."

I check Cho's leg with concern. "Are you really fit to go on?"

Cho nods. "I just need Renzo to throw up my grappling line."

I look Cho in the eyes. "I've already lost my mother," I whisper. "I don't want to lose you too."

She clenches her fist and raises it to me. "We made a battle-bond, remember? I'm in this till the end!"

We bump fists. "You're a true ninja," I say.

Renzo launches Cho's grappling line up the tower. The hook catches on the wall above. Renzo tests it with his weight. "We're good to go," he says.

I kick fresh snow over the mantrap and patches of blood. We must hide the fact that we have been here ... and escaped the trap.

Hand over hand, we begin to climb the castle wall.

In spite of her hurt leg, Cho pulls herself up the rope with the ease of a spider. Renzo and I wear *shuko* hand claws to climb the sheer rock-face.

We reach the stone-dropping holes. I cut the leather fastenings of a wooden hatch with my knife. When I peer in the open hole, I see a guard-room with a fire blazing in the grate. Next to the fire there is a large pile of rocks, ready to repel any attack.

The room appears to be empty.

Silently I clamber through the hole, followed by Cho and Renzo. We head over to the far door. But as we pass the rock pile, we come face to face with a samurai guard.

13. Stealth, Not Strength

The samurai is slumbering by the fire. I exchange uneasy glances with Cho and Renzo. The guard is a huge brute of a man with a bushy beard, but his eyes remain closed.

We creep across the room. The only noise is the snap and crackle of the fire.

Cho is almost at the door when I'm grabbed from behind and flung across the room. I crash head-first into the pile of rocks

I am stunned by the impact, and I can only watch as the bearded samurai swings a massive fist at Renzo.

Renzo ducks just in time and counters with a brutal punch to the samurai's gut. The strike would floor an ox, but the samurai doesn't seem to feel it. Renzo tries again, this time with a hook punch to the jaw. This time the samurai just laughs.

"You'll need to hit me harder than that, young ninja!"

The samurai seizes Renzo by the throat and lifts him off the ground. As Renzo struggles in the samurai's grip, he starts choking to death.

Then, without warning, the samurai

collapses to the floor.

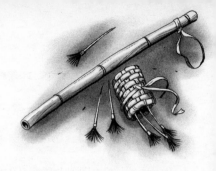

Cho stands behind, a blowpipe dart in her hand. "As the Grandmaster once said, why punch a rock when you can pierce a plum?" she says.

Renzo rubs his throat. "Thanks," he rasps.

"Now we're even," Cho says.

I get to my feet too. My head throbs from where it hit the rock pile, and I sway a little as I walk over to Renzo. Together we drag the samurai out of sight behind the rocks. He is still out cold. Then we leave the guard-room and hurry down a set of stone steps into an outer courtyard.

The crunch of marching feet alerts us

to a patrol. We dive into the doorway of a storehouse just as a unit of the Regent's samurai strides by. The samurai enter an inner gateway. They ignore the two sentries who open the gate for them.

As the patrol disappears, one of the sentries begins to complain. "Who do they think they are? Marching around as if they own the place."

The other sentry shakes his head in disgust. "They soon might. I hear the Regent is sending his entire army to wipe out the ninja."

The first sentry smiles. "Good. It's time we got rid of those scum. They're nothing but trouble."

When he hears this, Renzo takes out his

manriki chain. But I stop him before he can swing it.

"Stealth, not strength," I whisper.

I pick a pebble up off the ground and toss it to the far side of the courtyard. It hits a wall and clatters down a set of steps.

"Did you hear that?" says the first sentry. He peers into the darkness.

The other sentry nods. "I suppose we'd better take a look." He sighs. "Kenji ordered us to check out anything suspicious."

As they leave their posts, we sprint

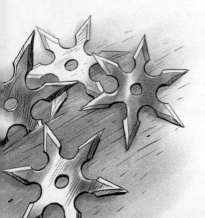

across to the gate. Cho tries the handle, but it won't turn. I take out my smallest *shuriken* and try to pick the lock with the thin spike.

"Hurry," Cho urges. "I can hear them coming back."

The footsteps in the snow get closer and closer.

In my rush, I drop the spike. As I scrabble to pick it up, Renzo tries the gate handle himself. With a firm push, the latch clicks opens.

Renzo smirks at Cho. "It just needed a little strength!"

We dart through the gate and close it behind us. The main tower of Black Eagle Castle looms over us as we cross an inner courtyard. We know from our last mission here that Lord Oda's rooms are on the third floor.

Renzo stops beside a high wall, leans against it and cups his hands. I put my foot into his hands and he boosts me over. I somersault through the air and land in

a garden on the other side. There's a pond surrounded by stone lanterns, bushes and a cherry-blossom tree.

As Cho drops down next to me, she lets out a gasp of pain. I see that her bandage is seeping blood.

"Are you all right?" I whisper.

"I'm fine," she says. She limps across the snow-covered garden towards the tower with her lips clamped together.

As I go to follow her, a short bald man with a round belly enters the garden. Cho disappears into the bushes, but I'm caught out in the open.

I freeze where I am. I don't even blink.

As the man strolls along the garden path, I recognise him. He is Lord Oda's adviser, Kenji. He looks straight at me ... then smiles.

"Ah! The gardener's made a snowman."

He chuckles. "But it needs a nose."

As Kenji bends down to take a pebble from the path, he catches sight of a patch of blood in the snow. His eyes follow the red trail to the bushes.

Kenji realises the danger and goes to cry out. "NIN–"

A dart pierces his neck and the word dies in his throat. Kenji collapses face-first in the snow.

Renzo lands beside me, silent as a leopard.

"Talk about hiding in plain sight," he says with a laugh.

I nod in agreement. "I don't think even the Grandmaster will believe it!"

Renzo helps me pull Kenji behind the cherry-blossom tree. Then he kicks the tree trunk and the adviser is buried in a shower of snow.

"Sweet dreams, samurai!" Renzo laughs again.

Cho limps out of the bushes, with her

blowpipe in her hand. While Renzo covers the blood trail, I tie a new bandage around her leg. She looks at the lumpy snow mound under the tree.

"We'd better move fast," she says. "It won't be long before someone realises he's missing."

We scale the main tower and enter by an open window on the third floor. The outer corridor is lit by oil lamps, but there's enough darkness for us to keep to the shadows.

We avoid a pair of samurai guards, then sneak around until we come to a long hallway that ends in a grand door. The door is decorated with a black eagle on top of a golden mountain.

"This must be Lord Oda's room," I whisper.

Cho stares down the hallway. "But why are there no guards?" she asks.

"They're probably on the other side," Renzo replies.

We're about to make our approach when the door slides open and a serving girl appears. I spot at least two of Lord Oda's bodyguards in the next room.

We retreat further into the shadows and watch as the serving girl shuffles down the hallway. I can hear the sound of birds chirping with her every step.

"*Uguisubari!*" Cho gasps, when the serving girl has gone. "A Nightingale Floor!"

Renzo and I look at her, confused.

"The Grandmaster once told me about these anti-assassin floors," she explains. "They're almost impossible to walk on without making a noise and alerting the guards."

"So how do we get across?" Renzo asks.

"*Uki-ashi*," Cho replies.

I shake my head in dismay. "Floating Feet! I haven't practised that type of stealth-walk in ages."

"Well, this is as good a time as any," Cho says.

Even with her wounded leg, Cho glides across the Nightingale Floor as silently as a ghost. Her feet don't even seem to touch the wooden boards.

Once Cho has reached the door, Renzo moves next. He's far heavier than me, but has had two more years of ninja training. He is slower than Cho, but he crosses the floor without making it 'sing' out.

Now it's my turn. I imagine myself as light as a feather and place my toes on the edge of the first floorboard. As I move my feet in a circular fashion and inch forwards, I never let my weight rest too long on one spot. That way I won't trigger the Nightingale Floor.

I feel a bead of sweat run down my brow as I glide across. I need every ounce of focus to 'float' my feet. Each floorboard is a new challenge. I have to sense its shape, where the danger spots are. I cannot pause for one second.

I'm nearly there ... two more boards to go ...

But then I rush my last step and the sound of a nightingale breaks the silence.

14. Broken Heart

A **bodyguard opens** the door and peers down the hallway.

"No one's there," he says to another guard.

I can see the top of the man's shaved head and I pray he doesn't look up. My arms shake as I hold myself between the wooden beams of the ceiling.

Renzo and Cho are next to me, and we

are all trembling with the effort of keeping ourselves up.

"Must have been that serving girl," the bodyguard says, and he slides the door shut.

With relief, we silently lower ourselves to the ground. Cho takes out her blowpipe and signals to me to get a *shuriken*. Renzo understands her plan, and he puts his fingers to the door and slides it open a crack. Cho slips the end of her blowpipe through …

Phut!

The dart flies across the room and strikes the first bodyguard. As he collapses to the floor, Renzo flings open the door and I throw my *shuriken* at the second bodyguard. Before the man can cry out a warning, the ninja star hits him in the throat. He slumps down beside his partner.

Now that we're in Lord Oda's private rooms, we have to move fast. Surprise is everything in an attack. I run to the opposite door and peek through to an inner chamber. The floor is covered with *tatami* straw mats. The paper walls are decorated with images of hunting birds – falcons, hawks and eagles.

This chamber is deserted, but a candle burns bright in the next room. Its glow casts a shadow of a kneeling man on the other side of the paper wall.

"I think I see him!" I hiss. I take out the
poisoned *shuriken* I've saved for my enemy.

Cho looks around the empty chamber. "This is too easy," she says.

But my eagerness gets the better of me.

I start to stealth-walk across the room. I pass a painting of a blue-black falcon ... then a swooping hawk ... then all of a sudden a painting of a golden eagle opens up and two bodyguards charge into the room.

Other panels spin open and six more guards appear, with their swords drawn.

Cho pulls out her own sword just in time to block an attempt to behead her. Renzo whips out his *manriki*.

"GO, TAKA!" Renzo cries, as he knocks out a samurai with the weight on one end

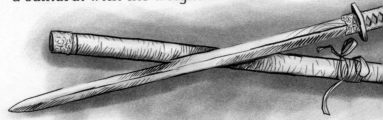

of his chain. "We'll hold them off!"

I leap aside to avoid a cruel slice from a bodyguard's sword. The tip of the blade just misses me, but it cuts into my bag. All my *shuriken* scatter across the floor.

I flick my last *shuriken* – the one meant for Lord Oda – at the bodyguard's right arm. It pierces his bicep and he drops his sword. The devastating side-kick I give him sends him flying through the paper wall into the next room.

On the other side of the ripped hole I see the scarred face of Lord Oda.

I step over the body of the guard and enter the room.

Lord Oda sits upon a raised platform, where he watches me without fear as I approach. In front of him is a short sword. But he makes no attempt to reach for it.

Now I have no *shuriken* left, I must get close enough to use the Death Touch. But this time Lord Oda won't survive the attack. For now I know where his heart really lies. Not on the left side of his body, like a normal man. But on the right.

"I knew you'd come," Lord Oda says. "You really are your father's son."

"You *murdered* my father!" I say. I feel my blood boil – although I was only a baby at the time and have no memory of it.

Lord Oda shakes his head. "That's not true."

"How can you say that?" I cry. "You killed my mother too."

"And I have suffered ever since that day," Lord Oda replies. His voice is heavy with sorrow.

The remorse that he claims makes me even angrier. Three months have passed since the battle to save our village, but I can still remember, clear as day, the moment Lord Oda thrust his blade into my mother.

I take another step forward and look at the sword lying between us. "Aren't you going to defend yourself?" I say.

"This sword isn't for you," replies Lord Oda. "It's for me to –"

Before Lord Oda can trick me with his snake words, I grab the sword to strike him down dead.

"I deserve to die," Lord Oda says, and he bows his head in surrender. "For I killed the woman I loved."

I stop the blade in mid-air. "W ... what?"

"Akemi. Your mother." He looks up at me and his eyes are red with tears. "Fifteen years ago, when I was a young samurai and not yet a lord, I met Akemi while I was out hunting in the mountains. Over that summer we fell in love. At the time I had no idea your mother was a ninja. And, to be honest, I wouldn't have cared."

I stand stock still. I can't believe my ears. But the truth is clear to read in the grief on Lord Oda's face. He means every word.

"Then why?" I ask. "If you were so in love with my mother, why do you want to destroy our ninja clan?"

"Because your clan leader destroyed our love!" he snarls. Anger flashes in his eyes and I take a step back.

"See this scar?" Lord Oda points to the red line that cuts across his right cheek. "Your old clan leader sent Akemi to kill the son of the new Lord of Black Eagle Castle. She had no idea that son was me. We fought in the dark, and her knife slashed my face. Then a shaft of moonlight let us see one another ..."

Lord Oda trembles as if he is haunted by the memory.

"We ... we cried in each other's arms at our tragic fate ... Akemi was faced with an impossible choice – me or the clan."

Lord Oda becomes choked with emotion and cannot speak. But his expression tells me more than he could ever say.

At last he manages to go on. "Your mother may not have killed me that night ... but she broke my heart. But I don't blame her. I blame the clan – and I always will."

Lord Oda looks at me, a sad yet tender smile on his face. "As Akemi died I heard her call your name. I couldn't believe it! We were going to call our first-born son ... Taka."

I drop the sword in shock. "You lie! I'm not your son."

"I know you are," Lord Oda replies. "How old are you now? Fourteen?"

I want to deny the truth. "I'm no samurai," I shout. "I'm a ninja!"

"You're both," he says with a short laugh. "Akemi's son the ninja. My son the samurai."

"But you murdered my father at the Battle of Black Eagle Castle."

"No, I killed your old clan leader. Your real father never died in that battle. But the night Akemi was sent to kill me, he did die here." Lord Oda points to where his heart is. "What was left turned rotten and hateful. But now I've lived to see you, my son, there is some light in the darkness."

I am stunned by all of this, frozen to the

spot. The sword lies at my feet, still within reach. Yet how can I kill my own father?

Angry shouts and alarm bells sound all over the castle.

Cho staggers into the room. "They must have found Kenji!" she cries. There is blood splattered across her white *gi*.

Renzo follows behind, a deep gash on his shaved head. He stares at the samurai lord in amazement. "Why haven't you killed him yet?" he demands of me.

I turn to my friends. "I can't ... He's my father," I say.

Cho and Renzo are shocked into silence.

Footsteps thunder up the castle's wooden stairs.

"You must go!" Lord Oda urges.

"If you're his father," Cho says, "then you can stop them."

Lord Oda shakes his head. "They're not my men to command," he replies. "The Regent's samurai are here for one purpose only – to wipe out every ninja in the land. But I can help you escape."

Lord Oda opens a wall panel to reveal a secret passage.

"This leads to the main gatehouse," he says. "Now go."

I have no choice but to trust Lord Oda. I duck into the passage with Cho and Renzo.

"Here, take this," says Lord Oda, and he hands me a scroll. "These are the plans for the

Regent's attack. I've had a change of heart –
use them to save your clan."

"Thank you ... Father."

Lord Oda smiles as if for the last time.
"Goodbye, my son."

15. In the Shadows

We exit the passage into the winch room of the castle.

Cho can barely walk. The fight with the bodyguards has taken its toll on her.

"Let me help you," I say, and I put an arm round her waist.

She's too weak to protest.

Renzo heads over to the winch, releases the catch and lowers the drawbridge.

The door bursts open and a samurai guard appears. "No one ordered the bridge to be –" He stops as his eyes widen in amazement at the sight of three blood-stained ninja.

The samurai draws his sword and charges at Renzo.

I reach into the pouch on my belt and throw the blinding powder into the man's eyes. He reels backwards, straight into the winch. One of its spinning handles smashes him on the head and he collapses to the floor.

"Time to go!" I say, as Renzo helps me to support Cho.

We stagger onto the drawbridge. In the courtyard behind, a unit of the Regent's samurai spots us.

"After them!" their leader orders.

The samurai rush towards us and they are fast gaining ground.

"You take Cho," Renzo says.

"But what about you?" I say.

"We made a battle-bond," he replies, holding up a clenched fist. "You saved my life. Now it's my turn to save yours."

He bumps his fist against mine, then turns to face the enemy.

"GO!" he shouts at me and Cho.

I carry Cho across the bridge and we stumble towards the forest. Behind us, I can hear the wasp buzz of Renzo's *manriki*.

"WHO'S FIRST?" he roars at the Regent's samurai.

As we reach the edge of the forest, I hear
a scream as someone falls into the gorge.

I look back in fear for Renzo. But he's still
standing on the bridge, battling the samurai.
That's the last I see of my brave and loyal
friend.

The fire crackles
in the hearth of
the Grandmaster's
temple. Cho and I warm ourselves by its heat.

Cho's leg rests on a cushion, and there
are fresh bandages round her wound. She
sips from a bowl of herbal soup that the
Grandmaster has made. She already looks
much better.

"So, it seems that Lord Oda is my father,"
I say, once I have told the Grandmaster the
whole story.

The Grandmaster nods. "Now I
understand why Akemi refused to go on any
more missions and became a healer instead."

I hand him the scroll that my father gave

me. The Grandmaster examines its wax seal with his fingertips.

"This is the real seal of the Regent!" the Grandmaster says in surprise. "These battle plans might just save the clan."

"We paid a heavy price for them," Cho says, and a tear rolls down her cheek.

We all bow our heads in honour of Renzo who gave up his life for us.

Then I turn to the Grandmaster. "Instead of always fighting, why can't there be a truce between ninja and samurai?" I ask.

The Grandmaster shakes his head. "The ninja and the samurai are as opposite as the moon

and the sun," he explains. "Just as night can never share the day, so the ninja will never be accepted by the samurai. But we will survive. For the ninja are warriors who live in the shadows."

Suddenly, a shivering youth steps out of the darkness.

"Renzo!" we exclaim in amazement and joy.

"Sorry I'm late," Renzo says, and he collapses by the fire.

I raise my fist in salute. Cho does the same and we all bump fists to make a battle-bond of three.

"To living in the shadows!" I say.

BLACK BUTTERFLY

CHO'S STORY

1. Float Like a Butterfly

Japan, Year 1581

I leap from the roof of the temple and land cat-like on the wall. It is dark, only a full moon to light my way. I tiptoe fast along the narrow wall. Behind me, I can hear the soft padding of feet.

Taka makes the leap from the roof to the wall. But he overshoots and nose-dives to the ground.

"It's all about balance," says the Grandmaster, who stands in the middle of the temple garden listening to our progress. "Float like a butterfly!"

The Grandmaster has set us an assault course challenge and I am in the lead.

When I reach the end of the wall, I have to make a tricky jump to a nearby tree. I fly through the air and land on a branch. It bends under my weight but doesn't break. With my arms outstretched, I scurry along. It is winter, there are no leaves on the tree, but my movement knocks an old bird's nest from above. It drops on my head and splits apart. As I shake off the dust and twigs, I feel something crawling on my neck.

Spider!

I hate spiders. I slap at it with my hand. But my foot slips and I lose my balance. I fall, crashing into branches on my way down, and I hit the ground hard. As I lie there groaning, I hear Renzo laugh in the tree above as he overtakes me. I sit up and rub my bruised ribs and watch the other ninjas complete the assault course.

The Grandmaster turns to me with his sightless eyes. "Not much floating there, Cho!"

"The most important element in the Art of Tea is getting the water temperature exactly right," the Grandmaster tells me the next day.

I sit beside him in his tea house, trying

not to let my attention wander. But out of a window I can see the other ninjas training with Sensei Kato. He's just shown them *uko* – "Door of Rain" – a nerve point on the side of the neck. Taka and Renzo are now practising this knockdown strike on each other. It looks a lot more fun than making tea!

The Grandmaster lifts the lid of the kettle and ladles hot water into a bowl before adding a scoop of tea leaves.

"Remember, every movement must be precise," he says. "You'll practise this over and over until it is perfect."

"Is this my punishment for failing the assault course?" I ask, picking up the ladle.

"No," the Grandmaster replies, a look of

surprise on his old face. "Why would you think that?"

"In the past week, you've made me learn to dance with fans, fold paper for origami, and now serve tea! Why can't I do the boys' training?"

The Grandmaster frowns. "Why learn something you already know? You're skilled in the art of fighting. Soon you'll be skilled in the art of tea-making."

With a cloth over the bowl, he pours tea into a small china cup, stopping before it gets to the brim. An impressive feat considering he is blind.

"But this is *so* boring," I say, trying not to yawn.

The Grandmaster lifts the cup to his lips, takes a sip and smiles.

"Your training is all about balance," he explains. "Like the assault course, if you don't balance the hard with the soft, the strong with the gentle, you will fall and *fail*."

"But why dancing and tea-making?" I ask. "These skills have nothing to do with being a ninja!"

"They have *everything* to do with being a ninja," the Grandmaster says, putting down his cup. "You'll need these skills for your next mission. A mission no boy can do."

I sit up straight. He has my full attention now.

"I want you to become a samurai," he explains.

"A *samurai*!" I cry in shock.

The Grandmaster nods. "You'll work as a serving girl in the Regent of Japan's castle in Kyoto and spy on Lord Kujo himself. As you know, he's vowed to wipe out every ninja in the land. We have his battle plans, but we need you to find out when he intends to attack."

Now my training makes sense. The tea-making, origami and dancing are all part of my disguise as a samurai serving girl. "I'll get my sword and black *gi*," I say, rising to my feet.

"No weapons!" the Grandmaster says. "No sword, no *shuriken*, no blowpipe. Nothing

that can identify you
as a ninja. You must
blend in like tea with
water."

"How will I defend myself?" I ask.

"With these," he replies. In his hand are a
gold hairpin and a paper fan.

I look at them in amazement. "But the
samurai will have swords and spears."

The Grandmaster twirls my long hair into
a bun and secures it with the pin. "Be careful
with this. The tip is sharpened and laced with
poison. It's as deadly as a spear and easier to
hide."

Then he hands me the fan.

"Will this give them a paper cut?" I joke.

The Grandmaster smiles. "It'll give them lot more than that. This is a *tessen*. The spine is made from steel. You can block swords and crack skulls with it."

I wave the fan in my hand. "But ... how do I use it?"

"Dance," he says.

Puzzled, I do as he asks. I dance about the tea house with the slow, flowing moves I learned in my lessons. I flick open the fan, twirl it in the air. I spin around, raise the fan up and sweep it back down.

"I don't see how this helps," I say.

"Dance faster," he replies.

When I do, the pattern in my moves suddenly becomes clear. Each pose is a block.

Each step, a thrust. Each arm motion, a strike. I realise now that to dance with the fan is to fight with it.

The Grandmaster points a bony finger at the colourful butterflies that decorate the fan.

"I'm told one of them is black," he says. "Be that black butterfly, Cho. Be invisible."

2. More Poet Than Warrior

One month later ...

"Any news from the scouting parties, Commander Hanzo?" Lord Kujo asks. He sits cross-legged upon a raised platform in the tea room of his castle.

The commander, a bearded man with a missing ear, shakes his bald head. "Nothing. The ninja have disappeared. It's as if they know our plans!"

I look down to hide my grin and focus on making tea for the two samurai and the boy who sits with them. But all the time I am listening and storing the information in my head.

"Send out more patrols," Lord Kujo orders. "I want to find and destroy the remaining ninja clans before the year is out."

"Why do we need to kill the ninja at all?" the boy asks.

Lord Kujo rolls his eyes. "Because they're our enemy."

"But there are so few left alive. How can they be a threat?"

"It only takes a small hole to burst a dam," Lord Kujo replies.

The boy looks thoughtful. "Wouldn't it be better to make peace with them? Then the dam would be stronger."

Lord Kujo and the commander burst into laughter.

"Make friends with the enemy?" Commander Hanzo snorts. "Mark my words, you can *never* trust the ninja. They're devils in black!"

Anger surges in me at his words and I struggle to hold my hand steady as I pour his tea.

"Hiro, you'll need more fighting spirit than that if you're going to rule one day," Lord Kujo warns. "Sometimes I wonder if you really are my son ..."

I notice the flush of shame in the boy's cheeks at his father's insult.

Lord Kujo takes a sip from his cup and remarks, "Perfect tea!"

The commander nods in agreement.

"What's your name, girl?" Lord Kujo asks, looking at me for the first time.

"Cho," I reply with a bow.

"That means butterfly," says Hiro, giving me a shy smile.

His father laughs. "See what I mean, Hanzo. He's more poet than warrior!"

Hiro blushes and the two samurai return to their battle plans. As they talk, I realise Hiro is staring at me. His eyes are brown like a deer's and his face is kind for a samurai.

I smile back at him and notice his cup is empty. As I go to refill it, my elbow knocks the commander's tea off the table.

I catch the cup before it falls to the ground. Not a single drop is spilt.

The commander's eyes narrow at me. "Fast reactions for a serving girl!"

I bow a silent apology and return to pouring more tea for Hiro.

As I hide in the garden bushes, an arrow flies past and strikes the target dead centre.

Commander Hanzo applauds Lord Kujo's archery skills. "You're a fine shot, my lord. The ninja stand no chance against you."

"Yes, we will crush them in battle!" says Lord Kujo, stringing another arrow.

The samurai's arrogance makes me sick. I've been spying on him for over a month now and all I want to do is jab my poisoned hairpin in his neck.

But my job is to spy, not to kill.

"I've good news," the commander continues. "A patrol has located a ninja clan in the Iga province."

My heart races. He's talking about *my* clan!

Lord Kujo fires his second arrow and splits the first in half.

"Call the generals together," he orders. "We must plan our attack."

I realise my clan's survival depends on me alone. I must find out their plan and then get a message to the Grandmaster fast.

"Found you!" cries a voice.

I spin around in surprise, my *tessen* held out to defend myself.

Hiro stares at the fan. "Sorry, I didn't mean to scare you," he says. "I just wanted to give you this *haiku*."

He hands me a piece of paper. I recover from my shock, lower my fan and read his poem.

Flapping and swaying
pretty butterfly dances
in the gentle breeze

"It's lovely," I say. No boy has given me

poetry before, and my heart warms to Hiro. I wish all samurai were like him.

"Your beauty inspires me," he says with his shy smile. "I've written more if –"

"Hiro!" calls Lord Kujo. "Stop talking to that serving girl and practise your archery."

Hiro sighs and looks at me. "It's always fight, fight, fight with my father." He begins to walk away, then stops and asks, "What were you doing in those bushes?"

I reply with an innocent smile. "I was collecting fresh herbs for your tea."

The night hides me as I climb the wall of the castle tower. I flit from stone to stone like a black butterfly. Near the top I peek through a window and spot Commander Hanzo's bald head. My arms ache as I cling on, but I must hear what Lord Kujo and his generals are planning.

"There are fewer than one hundred ninja left," the commander is saying. "We can easily destroy them."

As I listen, I feel something crawl up my arm. My blood freezes – it's a spider!

"Don't underestimate the ninja," says a general. "Remember how they defeated Lord Oda's army of one thousand soldiers?"

"Then we will bring *ten* thousand!" Lord Kujo says.

I try not to react as the spider creeps up my neck.

"So when do we attack?" Commander Hanzo asks.

Lord Kujo replies, "The first day of the cherry blossom."

The spider's now on my face. I can no longer stand it. I slap the creature away. But I lose my grip on the wall. As I slip, I snatch for the windowsill.

"What was that?" Commander Hanzo snaps. He thrusts his head out the window and looks around but sees nothing. "Must have been a bird."

Then he glances down and catches sight of my shadow hanging in the darkness.

"NINJA!" he shouts.

I let go and drop to the roof below. I hit the tiles hard, sliding towards the edge. At the last second I stop myself. Then I sprint along the roof.

The alarm has been raised. Torches are lit. Samurai run everywhere.

I leap from one roof to another. I must get to my room. Hanzo didn't see my face in the darkness, but if I'm missing from my bed, they'll know it was me.

I float through the air like a butterfly, land atop a wall and dash towards my room. I'm almost there when a troop of samurai enters the courtyard below. I jump into a tree and hide among the branches. When the guards are gone, I swing from a branch and through the open window into my room.

I've made it!

Then, turning to close the window, I spot Hiro in the courtyard.

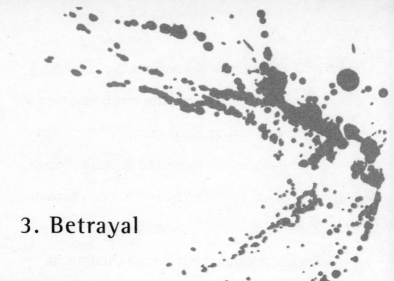

3. Betrayal

The next day ...

I am crushing herbs in the kitchen when two samurai guards seize me. They drag me before Lord Kujo.

"Is this who you saw last night?" he demands of his son.

Hiro nods.

Lord Kujo glares at me. "I sentence you to

224

death ..." He snarls. "By boiling."

The two guards haul me away and throw me into a cell. I slump against the bars of my prison in despair. I'm going to be boiled alive! Worse, I've failed in my mission. I can't warn my clan the samurai are coming.

Hiro's betrayal hurts too. I thought he liked me, perhaps even loved me. But I was fooling myself. He is samurai and I am ninja. We could never be together.

And tomorrow morning I'll be dead.

I start to weep.

A guard appears at the cell bars. "Oh, don't cry," he says softly. "We've a special meal tomorrow. Boiled ninja is on the menu!"

He laughs at his cruel joke.

Sobbing, I whisper to him.

"What did you say?" he asks, leaning in.

Once he's close enough, I pull out my hairpin and jab it into his neck. He grunts in pain, then sinks to the ground. The poison is fast-acting. And my tears a ninja trick to get his attention.

I reach through the bars, take his keys and open the cell door. As I sneak along the passage, another guard spots me and draws his sword. He attacks, his blade slicing down. I block it with my *tessen*, then smash the fan's tip on his head. He crumples to the floor.

I bound up the steps to flee the prison. My planned escape route takes me past the kitchens, then towards the secret gate at the

back of the castle. I'm almost there when I turn down a corridor and run straight into Hiro.

Before he can draw his sword, I shove him against the wall and hold the poisoned hairpin over his heart.

Hiro makes no move to defend himself. "Go on," he says, a tear rolling down his cheek. "You've already broken my heart."

"And you stole mine," I reply.

He looks deep into my eyes. "Why did I have to fall in love with a ninja?"

My hand trembles. "If you love me, why did you condemn me to die?"

"My father promised he wouldn't hurt you," Hiro says.

"And you say a ninja can never be trusted!" I sneer. "Samurai are the liars."

"I was coming to free you," says Hiro, showing me the heavy key in his hand. "I could never let you die."

He is telling the truth and I surrender to my feelings. I drop the hairpin and kiss Hiro on the lips. What does it matter that he is samurai and I am ninja?

Hiro wraps his arms around me and holds me tight. All is forgotten and all is forgiven. Then shouting and the sound of running footsteps breaks the moment between us. The dead prison guards have been discovered.

"Go!" Hiro says, urging me towards the gate. "Go before it's too late."

"It's already too late," Commander Hanzo growls, striding towards us and drawing his sword. "Your father will hear of your betrayal, Hiro!" he snarls. "But first I'll execute this ninja spy."

His sword slices to cut off my head. But Hiro steps into its path.

The blade stops a hair's breadth from his neck.

"Get out of my way!" roars Hanzo. He kicks out at Hiro and sends him crashing to the floor.

Rage consumes me and I raise my *tessen* to attack.

The commander laughs. "What! Are you going to *fan* me to death?"

"I may float like a butterfly, but I sting like a bee!" I reply, slamming the steel edge against his sword arm. There's a sharp crack as a bone breaks.

Screaming in pain, Hanzo drops his sword. I swing the fan tip at his bald head, but he ducks and barges me into the wall. The impact stuns me. With his other hand, Hanzo draws his short sword.

"Die ninja girl!" he shouts, thrusting the blade at my heart.

I deflect the attack with my fan, then strike at a nerve point in his neck – *uko*, "Door of Rain".

Hanzo crumples to the floor. But he's

only knocked out. I spot a glint of gold at my feet. I snatch up the hairpin and go to stab the commander in the neck.

"NO!" Hiro cries, grabbing my wrist.

"But he saw us together!"

"No killing," Hiro insists. "I'll deal with Hanzo myself. Let's hope his memory is hazy after the blow."

"Hiro, come with me," I plead as I hear guards approach.

"I can't." Hiro shakes his head. "This castle is my home. Just as your home is with your ninja clan." He takes my hand in his. "But maybe one day, when I am Regent of Japan, we can share the same home."

The guards are almost upon us.

"Now, Cho, *run!*" Hiro cries as he kisses me one last time.

I disappear through the gate.

4. Heart Over Head

The sun is setting behind the mountains by the time I reach my village. The Grandmaster is waiting for me in the temple. I tell him about Lord Kujo's planned attack.

The Grandmaster turns to face the darkness. "We cannot fight ten thousand men. We must find a new place to hide, a place to live in the shadows. But this time we'll disappear for ever."

The thought of leaving and never returning breaks my heart.

"But what about Hiro?" I say. "He wants to make peace with us."

"Hiro is not the Regent yet," the Grandmaster reminds me. "And he is still a samurai. He may love you, but his loyalty lies with them, not you."

"He's *not* the same as other samurai," I insist.

"Don't let your heart rule your head," the Grandmaster warns me.

"But what," I cry, "about love?"

The Grandmaster sighs. "It's true. Love is a power greater than sword, samurai or ninja. Perhaps one day – with more young people like you and Hiro – ninja and samurai will find a way to live in harmony. But until then we ninja must be warriors in the shadows."

The Grandmaster walks away until the dusk swallows him.

I sit on the temple steps all alone. And, as the last light fades, I think of Hiro. He is the sun. I am the stars. Only at dusk and dawn do night and day ever meet.

But there's hope in my heart ... for, in the day, light creates the shadow.

YOU NEED THE RIGHT KIT TO SUCCEED AS A NINJA.

How well do you know your ninja kit?

1. What is a shuriken?

    a. A double-edged sword

    B. A throwing star

    C. A poison dart

2. What is a gi?

    a. A ninja outfit

    B. A pair of ninja shoes

    C. A special ninja bag

3. Why is a ninja black belt important?

    a. Because it means you have just started ninja training

    B. Because now you are ready for any ninja mission

    C. Because it stops your ninja trousers falling down

4. **What two things make Tenshin's Sword of Destruction so special?**

   a. It has a "blood groove" so you can pull it out of your enemy's body more easily

   B. It is so heavy it takes three ninja to lift it

   C. Its edge is sharp and jagged like a saw

5. **What is a manriki?**

   a. A set of poison darts in a hollow tube

   B. A heavy steel chain

   C. A silk fan with a sharp point

6. **What does a ninja need to hide in plain sight?**

   a. A thick woollen cloak

   B. A snowman costume

   C. Nothing special

7. **Where might a ninja use a pair of ashiaro?**

   a. On their feet to make animal footprints in the snow

   B. On their eyes to protect them from snow-blindness

   C. On their hands to climb a steep wall or tree

ANSWERS: 1B; 2A; 3B; 4A+C; 5B; 6C; 7A

Have you got what it takes to be a true ninja?

Take the Grandmaster's quiz and find out.

1. In an emergency, what is your motto?

a. "Help! Mum! Help!"

B. "We made a battle-bond. I'm in this till the end."

C. "Who Dares Wins!"

2. Who do you count as your best friends?

a. Everyone – ninja, samurai, serving girls, the Regent of Japan ...

B. A few trusted ninja, and the Grandmaster for his wisdom.

C. No one. A ninja always acts alone.

3. "Why punch a rock when you can pierce a plum." What does this mean?

a. It always pays to carry a selection of fresh fruit with you.

B. Choose your weapons wisely.

C. Sometimes it's best to hit someone as hard as you can.

4. If you have to cross a nightingale floor, what do you do?

a. Sprint as fast as you can and hope for the best.

B. Call on your "floating feet" skills, which you practise every day.

C. Scale the nearest wall and hang upside down from the ceiling.

5. Which of these are true words of wisdom from the Grandmaster?

a. Never assume a man with no eyes cannot hear.

B. A ninja must never do what his enemy expects.

C. It doesn't matter how slowly you go, as long as you speed up at the end.

Have you got what it takes to be a true ninja

Answers

Mostly As: White Belt

Have you been paying attention? You still have a lot to learn from your ninja training. But remember, failure is success if you learn from it.

Mostly Bs: Black Belt

You are a true ninja. But be careful how you go, for a small error is as deadly as a big one.

Mostly Cs: Red Belt

You are always ready for action, but need to work on your "stealth not strength" training before you become a true ninja.

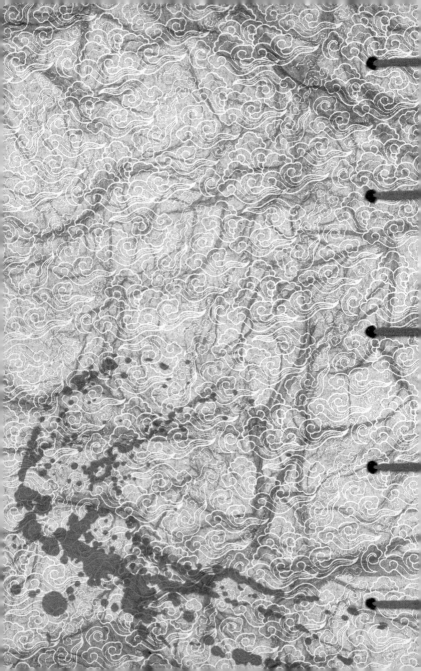

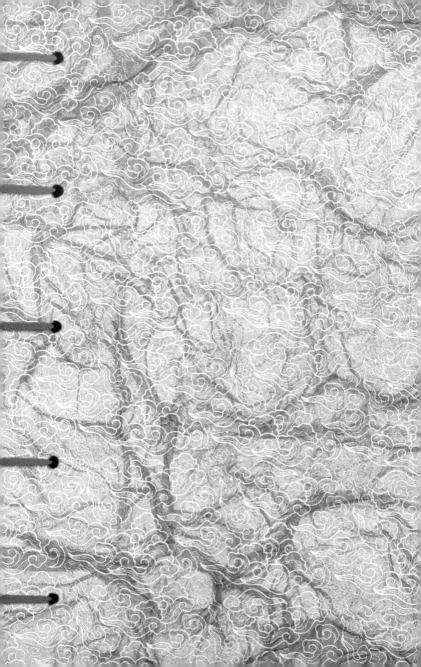

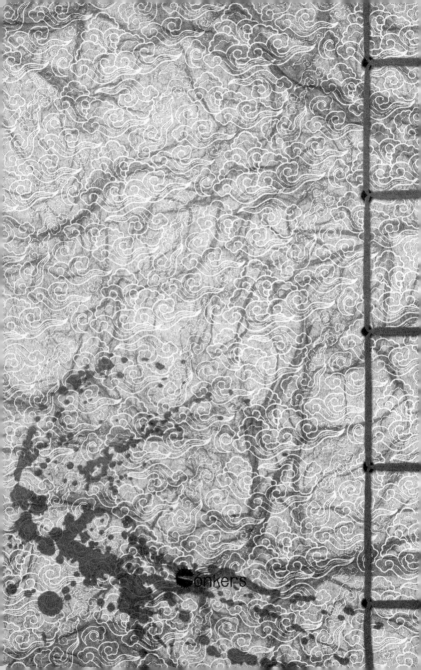
Conkers